MW01241906

Allison

by Jean Varner

PublishAmerica
Baltimore

First printing

ISBN: 1-4137-0602-9
PUBLISHED BY PUBLISHAMERICA, LLLP
www.publishamerica.com
Baltimore

Printed in the United States of America

In Dedication

To my husband Bill
and to our children
Michael, David, Patricia, Mary, and Stephen

Psalm 127:3

Prologue

Chicago, Illinois
April 1968
Sylvia's thoughts were in a turmoil as she left the doctor's office. Cancer! The doctor said the reports had come back and the tumor was malignant! She had been so sure it would be okay. He mentioned treatment, but she wanted to wait until she could tell her husband. Bernie would come with her the next time and help her decide.

She glanced at her reflection in the store window as she passed and saw a defeated stranger. The elegant business suit clothed a hunched-over slender figure, drooping along. Neatly coifed, brown hair framed a sad, depressed face. She straightened up into her usual self-assured stride. No! Cancer would not defeat her. All of her colleagues and friends knew her as a strong person. Sylvia Ashley Bachman was a survivor!

Yet, the devastation in her gray eyes lingered.

Since she didn't feel up to facing people, she entered the side-door of her office building and took the stairs. On the fourth floor she walked down the hall to the door with the names of Borden, Ashley, and Lee, Attorneys-at-Law printed on the frosted glass. She took out her key, unlocked the door, and entered the empty offices. Good, she thought, everyone was still at lunch. After locking the door she passed through to her private office and shut the door. Then she collapsed into her desk chair.

The doctor hadn't held out much hope for her. With treatment, she might expect to live two years, he had said. She folded her arms on her desk and laid her head on them. A few tears seeped from under her closed lids and slid down her cheeks.

"Oh, Lord," she prayed, "let me see my daughter once more before I die."

Twenty-three years earlier, Sylvia had borne a baby out of wedlock

5

and had given her up for adoption. She had never told her parents. After the delivery, things went wrong and a hysterectomy had been necessary to save her life.

Before the baby was taken away and given to the adoptive parents, they allowed Sylvia to hold her. She was a beautiful baby with a mop of thick, black hair and a round, cherubic face. The baby opened her large, dark eyes and stared into her mother's face as if trying to memorize it. Of course Sylvia knew newborns couldn't see, but she talked to her and told her she loved her and wished she could keep her. It was doubly hard to give her up since it was the only baby she would ever have.

Her thoughts turned to the tall, handsome airman who had fathered her child. She had loved him so much, but he had only used her and left her pregnant.

She straightened up as she heard the voices of the others returning from lunch. She wiped her eyes and quietly blew her nose. Pulling some papers out of her in-box she pretended to read. The door opened and Debbie, her secretary, entered.

"Oh, Ms. Ashley, I didn't know you were here. The hall door was still locked."

"I wanted some privacy until you returned," Sylvia said. "I have a lot of work to catch up on. I'll eat later."

Shortly after Debbie shut the door, the telephone rang. A few minutes later, her buzzer sounded. She pressed the intercom button and said, "Yes?"

"A man is on the phone and wants to speak with you. He said his name is John Hook."

Her thoughts ran wild. John Hook! The father of her child. She had just been thinking about him. The man who had nearly ruined her life.

"Ms. Ashley, are you alright?" Debbie sounded concerned.

"I'm okay. Put him on."

Her heart fluttered as the familiar baritone voice from her past came on the line. "Are you the Sylvia Ashley that I met in Oklahoma City during the forties? I was in the air force and was stationed there."

"Yes, I am. What can I do for you?"

"I saw your name in the paper as the lawyer in a certain case and wondered if you were the girl I once knew. Why don't we eat lunch together and talk over old times?"

Sylvia was shocked. The nerve of him. Acting as if their parting had been casual. Well, it probably was for him. One Friday afternoon he had taken her to Dallas on the pretext that they would be married. It was too late to get a license. She had been surprised when he booked only one room, but she had trusted him. The next day he said they couldn't get a license because it was Saturday, but they would be married Monday in Oklahoma City. They spent another night in Dallas. He took her back to her apartment Sunday afternoon, and that was the last time she saw him. When she couldn't reach him, she had called one of his married friends who lived off base, and he told her that John had been shipped out.

"Sylvia?"

"I was thinking about 'old times.'"

"Those were great days when we were young."

"Do you live in Chicago?"

"No, I'm here on business from Dayton, Ohio. How about lunch?"

Suddenly she made up her mind. "Okay, meet me at Don's Bar and Grill. It's near my office."

"I'll take a taxi and be there in twenty minutes."

She called her secretary in and said, "I'm going to lunch with an old acquaintance. Probably be gone an hour."

Sylvia deliberately waited to leave so he would arrive first. When she entered the dimly-lit grill, she looked around and saw John at the bar with a drink in front of him. She recognized him immediately. For a few minutes she observed him as he flirted with the barmaid.

Approaching him slowly she could hear the line he was feeding the girl. He hadn't changed a bit, she decided.

"Hello, John," she said softly.

He turned around quickly and took both her hands in his while he surveyed her with his intense brown eyes. "Sylvia! You look great!"

Age had not diminished his handsome face. The gray around the edges of his black hair gave him a distinguished appearance. His waistline might have been a bit thicker, but his expensive suit covered it well. He led her to a small table in the corner of the room and pulled out a chair for her.

After the waitress brought the menu and they had ordered, he said, "So, you've become a lawyer and, from what I hear, a very sharp one. How did I ever let you slip through my fingers?"

Sylvia wondered if she should tell him about the baby, but decided to wait. Instead she asked about his job. He told her he was a salesman for a construction company and was here to drum up business.

Under closer inspection she noticed the lines of dissipation that showed on his face. He had ordered wine with his meal while she settled for iced tea. While they ate, she listened to him drone on and on about himself and decided he had turned into an egotistical bore. How could she have not noticed that while dating him?

Finally she asked him if he was married.

He laughed and said, "Yeah, I've married three times, but it's never worked out.

Haven't found the right one yet. Hah! I may ask you to help me get rid of my present wife. I'll need a good lawyer. Are you married? I notice you have a wedding band and a large diamond, but you still go by Ashley."

"Yes, I'm married to a wonderful man, but I keep Ashley as my professional name. Do you have children?"

"Yes, five. Two by my first wife, one by my second wife, and two by my present wife." Then he laughed and said, "And I don't know how many 'other ones' I have, if you get my meaning."

At these callous words, Sylvia seethed with anger. Before she could say anything, he asked her for a date—dinner, dancing, and who knows what else.

She stood up and lifted her tea glass in the air and said, "A toast to the 'other ones.'," and threw the iced tea in his face.

While he sat dripping wet with an astonished expression, she put a twenty dollar bill on the table and walked out.

"That toast is for you, Allison," she whispered.

Chapter 1

Chicago, Illinois
April 1970

Heads turned as Allison Ames crossed the foyer to the elevators of a Chicago office building. She was accustomed to the stares of others and paid no attention. A strikingly beautiful woman, she was tall and statuesque with shoulder-length black hair, a fair complexion, and large luminous brown eyes. Her fashionable black suit fit to perfection, and a string of pearls with matching pearl earrings added to her elegant appearance. Her only other jewelry was a solid gold band on the third finger of her left hand. Entering the elevator she glanced at the white business card in her hand and then punched the button for the seventh floor.

When she stepped off the elevator, she turned left and walked down the hall until she came to the law offices of Connel and Estes. As she paused with her hand on the door handle, a soft whistle caused her to turn her head. She looked into the smiling eyes of a young man in a business suit. He grinned appreciatively at her and then passed her and walked jauntily down the hall.

Allison opened the door and entered the reception room. A small matronly woman sat at a desk. The nameplate on her desk read Dot Pierce.

"May I help you?" the woman asked.

"My name is Allison Corley Ames, and I have an appointment with Mr. Estes."

"Oh, yes, he's expecting you." Ms. Pierce pushed the button on her intercom and announced, "Mrs. Ames is here to see you." Indicating the door behind her, she said, "You may go in."

Allison entered an impressive office containing a massive mahogany desk and maroon leather chairs. Bookcases filled with law books lined one wall. A thick gray carpet covered the floor, and maroon drapes hung at the large windows.

Mr. Estes, a tall spare man with sparse gray hair, appeared to be in his late fifties. He came forward, took both her hands in his and said, "Allison Corley! You were a beautiful baby, and you have grown up to be a beautiful woman. We were sorry to hear of the death of your mother. How is your father?"

"Thank you," she said in a soft voice. "Dad is taking a three-month leave from work to cruise the Mediterranean with my aunt and uncle on their yacht. They plan to spend time on different Greek islands. Mother's long and painful illness was stressful for him, and he needed to get away for a while."

"It sounds like a good idea," he said as he seated her in a leather chair and then sat down behind the desk.

"You have a two-year-old son, is that right?" he asked.

"Yes. A friend is keeping him today. His name is Corley."

"After your maiden name. It makes a nice name, Corley Ames. I understand that you lost your husband in Vietnam? A terrible war!"

"Yes." She sat twisting her ring and said, "I can't bear to part with this yet."

"You've had your share of deaths, but I must tell you of one more. Your birth mother died a month ago. I didn't want to tell you over the phone."

"Oh, no!" she cried. "After my mother's death, I had the urge to find her, and Dad gave me your card. Now it's too late!"

"She had wanted us to let her know if you ever asked to meet her, but when she knew she was dying of cancer, she gave us this letter for you." He handed her a business-size envelope with "Allison" written on it in a bold, but feminine hand.

Allison took the envelope and stared at it with tears in her eyes. Without looking up she asked in a low voice, "What was her name?"

"Sylvia Ashley Bachman. She was an attorney in a prestigious law firm, and she went by her maiden name professionally."

Allison looked up in surprise. "Sylvia Ashley? I've heard of her, and I've seen her picture in the papers!"

"Yes, she was a brilliant lawyer."

"And my father?"

"She never mentioned his name. Just said he wouldn't be involved."

Allison rose to go, and Mr. Estes got up quickly to open the door for her. "Sorry I had to give you bad news," he said.

"And I'm sorry I waited too long to get in touch with her. Thank you for seeing me."

Allison went into the parking garage next door. Her maroon Ford Mustang was parked near the rear on the ground floor. The light was dim. She got in the driver's seat and looked at the envelope. Carefully she opened it and removed a folded sheet. A small packet fell out into her lap. Enclosed in it was a child-size gold ring with a heart-shaped ruby setting. She turned on the overhead light and saw the initials S.A. engraved on the inside of the band. Tearfully she unfolded the letter and read:

Dear Allison,

What a lovely name. Allison. I know you are as lovely as your name. If I could put my arms around you and tell you how much I love you, my joy would be complete.

The hardest thing in the world I ever did was to give you up for adoption. It broke my heart, but I knew you would be better off in a two-parent home. At the time I was only eighteen and had nothing but love to offer you. Maybe it would have been enough, but for your sake, I could not risk it.

If you ever read this, I will be in heaven. The Lord has forgiven my sins. My work as an attorney has been very satisfying, and I have had a good life with a loving husband. It is clear to me that you have had a happy home. Every year on your birthday, your parents sent me a picture of you through my lawyers.

Enclosed is the ring my parents gave me as a child. It is proof for them that you are my daughter. I never told them that I had a child out of wedlock. Maybe now that I am gone, they will be glad to have a grandchild, since I was their only child.

If you want to get in touch with them, and I hope you will, I am giving you the name and address of one of my best friends. She will be glad to help you.
With all my love,
Your mother,
Sylvia Ashley Bachman

On a separate slip of paper was the name and address and phone number of Meg Sullivan in Oak Grove, Oklahoma.

By the time Allison finished reading the letter, tears ran unheeded down her cheeks. If only she had tried to meet her birth mother sooner! She turned off the light, laid her head on the steering-wheel, and sobbed quietly.

At times during her childhood she had wondered why her birth parents had given her away. It made her feel rejected. She hated them for it. Once her mother found her crying and when she told her the reason, her mother explained that her birth parents loved her enough to want the best for her. At the time she couldn't understand, but as she grew older it became clearer to her. While in her teens she thought about trying to find them, just to learn the reason why they abandoned her. She never followed through with her plans. Now it was too late. From this letter she realized how much her birth mother had loved her. Her tears were for her mother as well as for herself.

Deep in her grief, she paid no attention to a car that passed by and parked two spaces down from her. She vaguely heard the opening and closing of car doors.

The sound of two men talking in low guttural voices nearby roused her. She raised her head and looked in their direction, but could only see their outlines in the shadows. One was tall and slender and the other short and stout.

"Are you sure he's gonna be here at one-thirty?" one asked.

"Of course I am. I told you I had 'ears' in the police station," the other one responded. "Shhh! Here he comes."

One of them stepped out of the shadows and stood directly under a light. He was a tall, rangy man with a long face and hard blue eyes. In his right hand he held a gun!

Gripped by terror, Allison gasped and ducked down into the car. Had the man with the gun seen her? Her stomach twisted in knots. Any moment she expected him to peer over the side of the door. She squeezed her eyes shut and trembled.

"What are you doing here?" a new voice asked. "You're not the one I'm supposed to meet."

"Well, the plans have been changed. You've been found out, so they sent me."

Allison heard the rustling of sudden movement. Then the dull whisper of the silencer on the gun and a whack as it hit its target. Stunned, she dug her fingers into the leather car seat. Fearfully she waited for the pressure of the gun against her head.

Instead she caught the sound of car doors opening and closing and the purr of a motor starting up. After the car passed her, she cautiously raised her head. It stopped for a few seconds at the exit booth while the driver paid the fare. The license tag was lighted and she could read the numbers. Groping in her purse she pulled out a pen and jotted them on the envelope of her letter. She wanted to leave the scene quickly, but she needed to see if she could aid the victim. Her legs felt like jelly as she crawled out of the car. She clung to the door for a few seconds until strength returned to them. Dreading what she would find, she peered around her car. The body of a young man lay sprawled on the cement floor. The bullet had gone through the middle of his forehead. Blood had seeped from under his head and stained the pavement. He was dead! Nauseated, she stumbled back to the car. Fumbling the key in the lock, she finally started the motor and pulled out. At the exit, she paid her parking-ticket, and the young attendant grinned at her and said, "Come back again, Beautiful!"

When Allison was a few blocks away, she heard sirens. Her hands trembled on the steering-wheel. The body must have been found! Would the young attendant remember her? She must get away fast. The killer had said that they had 'ears' in the police station. One of the policemen must be a spy. If she told the police that she had witnessed the crime, the killer would find out! She didn't slow down until she reached her apartment. Quickly she changed into a pair of jeans and a plaid shirt, combed her hair back into a pony-tail, and packed clothes for herself and Corley. On the way out, she dropped a stop-the-mail note in the mailbox, and then drove to the bank and cashed a sizable check. She would pay cash and not use her credit card.

Upon entering her friend's apartment, she was dismayed to find Corley with a fever.

"He was listless and didn't eat his lunch," Elna Evans said, "so I took his temperature. It was 102 degrees. You'd better take him to his doctor."

"I will," Allison said, nervously.

"Are you ill, too, Allison? You look so pale and distraught."

"I just found out that my birth mother is dead. I hoped to look her up and get acquainted. It affected me worse than I thought it would. It was a shock to find that she died about the same time as my adoptive mother did."

"I'm so sorry, Allison. You were looking forward to meeting her, weren't you? Is there anything I can do for you?"

"No. Thanks anyway. I'd better get going."

"Yes, you need to get Corley to the doctor. Let me know what you find out."

"Okay," Allison said as she picked up Corley and headed for the car. His eyes were closed, and his silky black lashes lay in half-moons on his flushed cheeks. When she spoke his name softly, his brown eyes opened, and he smiled sleepily at her. She placed him in his car seat in the back.

A few blocks down the street, she stopped at a drugstore and bought babyaspirin and a bottle of water. After he swallowed the dropper full of sweet-tasting medicine and thirstily drank the water, she drove on. Frequently she glanced at the cars behind her. Was that long black car following her? The terrible scene in the garage was still fresh in her mind. She shuddered.

It was after four when she reached the outskirts of the city and pulled over to a pay phone to call the police. Briefly she told the woman who answered the phone that she had seen two men shoot a third one in a parking garage and gave her the license tag number. Before the operator could ask any questions, she hung up the receiver. She was afraid to give her name. One of the policemen was an informant for the killers.

On Interstate 55 she had her car filled with gas at a service station and bought a map of Oklahoma. Corley woke up dripping wet with his black curly hair plastered to his head, but he was not as listless as he had been. She dried him off in the restroom and put fresh clothes on him. In the deli at the service station she bought chicken noodle soup, and he ate a little of it and drank more water.

Late that night she reached Springfield, Illinois and stopped at a motel. Corley's temperature was rising again, so she gave him another dose of aspirin. He slept well, but Allison had a restless night. Suddenly, she heard the window open. Paralyzed with fear, she saw a dark figure climb through the window. He crept closer and closer until he was by her bed. Her heart beat erratically. The night-light shone on the long face and cold eyes of the killer! She tried to scream, but no sound came out. He pointed his gun at her and fired. She awoke with a start. It took several seconds for her to realize it was a nightmare. Her bed was drenched with perspiration.

There was no more sleep for her that night. She got up and showered, then packed her bags. Corley slept as she carried him to the car and placed him in his car seat. During the morning she stopped at a restaurant for breakfast, but Corley would only drink orange juice and water. She tried to tell herself that she was only imagining the murderers would follow her. After all, they hadn't seen her. But she still wanted to put as much distance as she could between herself and them.

At St. Louis she took Interstate 44 across Missouri toward Oklahoma. As she drew closer to her destination, concern swept over her about what kind of a welcome she would receive from Meg Sullivan. She had been in such a hurry to get away that she hadn't taken time to call and let her know she was coming. Even though she still had time to phone she feared to let anyone know her whereabouts. Never had she forced herself on anyone the way she was about to do on this woman. Maybe Oak Grove had a motel where she could stay. If circumstances had been different, and she hadn't witnessed that murder, she would have waited a few days to decide whether to go or not. However, she had felt compelled to leave the area as quickly as possible.

Corley slept as the miles flew by. When he felt warm and became restless, she gave him aspirin and all of the water, orange juice, and soda he would drink. The aspirin brought his temperature down and caused him to perspire. Several times she had to change his clothes. Although she was worried about him, she still pressed on. She would take him to a doctor the first thing when they got to Oak Grove.

After they crossed into Oklahoma, she stopped to consult her map and turned south on State Highway 10. The further south she drove, the more rugged the terrain became. She had always thought of Oklahoma as a flat treeless plain, but this was beautiful country with winding roads and wooded hills. However, she was too worried and scared to admire the view. Also it took a lot of time on this two-lane curving highway. A bridge crossed over the Grand Lake of the Cherokees at the town of Grove. There she caught Highway 59 and stayed on it.

They spent the night in a motel in Sallisaw, Oklahoma. She was afraid to go to sleep. Would she dream of the killer again? Why was that man killed? Who was he? The thought hit her. She would be dead right now if they had seen her! A heavy tiredness finally overcame her and she dropped off to sleep.

Early the next morning she was up and on her way again. Around ten a.m. she turned onto the county road that led into Oak Grove. She hesitated briefly, but one look at Corley told her his condition had worsened. She feared for him and knew she had to get him to a doctor at once. Would there be one in Oak Grove?

Had her flight endangered her baby's life?

Chapter 11

Oak Grove, Oklahoma
April 1970

When the alarm went off on the clock radio at the bedside table next to Meg, she ignored it. Her husband, Joe, leaned across her to turn it off.

"Wake up, Sleepyhead," he whispered in her ear.

When that didn't work, he playfully whacked her on the bottom.

"Ouch! You're a beast," she muttered, although she barely felt the blow through the covers. She turned on her back, stretched, and eyed her handsome husband. He was out of bed with his pajama top off heading for the bathroom. At forty-eight he still had broad shoulders, a flat abdomen, and muscular arms and legs. As yet, no white appeared in his crisp black hair.

"Isn't this your morning to fix breakfast?" she teased.

He turned around and grinned at her. "In your dreams," he said. She loved the way his grey eyes lit up when he was happy. They were a legacy of his Irish father and contrasted with his dark skin. His mother had been Indian and most of his features were from her forebears--- black brows that nearly met over a high-bridged nose, high cheekbones, full lips, and a firm chin.

When Meg heard the shower running, she got out of bed and slipped into her robe and house slippers. Looking in the mirror, she combed her short curly brown hair and then leaned forward to examine her face. No age lines showed yet and her blue eyes were as bright as ever.

Downstairs, as she passed through the hallway, she rapped on each of the bedroom doors of her children and called their names, "Sarah, Jimmy, Sammy, Callie. Rise and shine."

By the time they entered the kitchen, a large platter of crisp fried

17

bacon, stacks of golden toast, butter and jelly, and a large bowl of oatmeal were on the table. Family devotionals followed the meal. Joe read a passage of scripture, and all of them participated in discussing or asking questions about what they had heard. When it was time to leave for school, Joe kissed Meg and the children called their goodbyes as they piled into the pickup.

Meg took a leisurely shower, dressed, and then cleaned the house. For lunch she prepared a light salad. Her figure was a little fuller than when she had married, but there wasn't an ounce of fat on it. It hadn't been easy keeping it off after five babies, but she was determined not to get plump like her friend Sue.

As she finished eating, she heard Max, the family's black Labrador retriever, bark at a car coming up the drive.

"Who can that be?" she wondered as she crossed the room to open the door.

A dusty maroon Mustang with a bug-spattered windshield pulled in the driveway and stopped. A tired-looking young woman in rumpled jeans and shirt, with her untidy black hair straggling out of a pony-tail, climbed out of the front seat.

"Are you Meg Sullivan?" she asked.

"Yes, I am," Meg replied. "May I help you?"

"I'm Allison Corley Ames, Sylvia Ashley's daughter, and I do need help."

"You are most welcome," Meg said, as she went to the car and hugged her. "I see the resemblance in the pictures of you that Sylvia gave me. What can I do for you?"

"My baby is ill and I need a doctor."

Meg saw the baby in the back seat of the car and said, "Bring him in and I'll call my family physician, Dr. Newberry."

She held the door open while Allison carried the sick child in and laid him on the couch. His eyes remained closed, his face was pale, and his breathing was labored. A blue tinge appeared around his mouth.

"Oh, dear, he's very sick," Meg said and hurried to the phone.

After she talked to the receptionist, she turned to Allison and said,

"Dr. Newberry is out on a maternity case, but his assistant, Dr. Doug Gregory, said to bring him down to his office right away. I'll take you in my car. It'll be faster."

When they reached the doctor's office they were taken immediately into an examining room. Dr. Gregory, a tall, handsome man in his early thirties, with brown curly hair and gray eyes, came in at once. He had a brusque manner and shook his head when he saw the baby. After he listened to the child's chest, looked in his throat, eyes, and ears, he asked Allison if he had any allergies. When she said she didn't know of any, he instructed the nurse to give him an injection of penicillin.

"How long has he been like this?" he asked.

"He had a fever when I picked him up at my friend's apartment day before yesterday," she admitted.

"Why didn't you take him for treatment then?" he demanded.

"I-I was in a hurry to leave town."

"He has pneumonia, and we're going to have to put him in the hospital right away, and it'll be touch and go for a while. Was your haste worth your baby's life?" he asked.

Allison's face blanched. "Oh, no, no!" she cried, but Dr. Gregory had already left the room to call the hospital in the nearby town of Wolfeton.

The nurse gave Corley an intra-muscular injection and then put a mask attached to a small tank of oxygen over his face.

Dr. Gregory returned and said, "We'll go in my car instead of calling the ambulance. You sit in the back seat with him and keep the oxygen mask on him."

"Alright," Allison said with tears in her eyes.

"I'll go get your suitcases and call my husband," Meg said. "Then I'll come straight to the hospital and stay with you."

While at home she called Joe and told him the situation and added, "Tell Sarah to warm up leftovers, unless you want to take them out to the drive-in for hamburgers. I won't be back until morning."

Meg left the bag of soiled clothes in the laundry room to be washed at a later time and put the two suitcases in her station-wagon. At the hospital she stopped at the information desk and asked for Corley's room number. As she turned to pick up the bags, a redheaded orderly took them from her and carried them to the room. Meg tried to tip him, but he wouldn't let her.

"I don't like to see a pretty lady carry heavy luggage," he said with a grin and hurried off.

Corley lay in an oxygen tent with intravenous fluids running into a vein in his hand which was bound to a small covered board. Allison stood beside his crib sobbing. Meg took the young mother in her arms and tried to comfort her.

"Oh, Meg," she cried, "I'm a terrible mother. Why didn't I realize how ill he was and take him to a doctor sooner?"

"Allison, you're not a terrible mother. I can tell your baby has had good care. Dr. Gregory shouldn't have talked to you that way, and I'll tell him so."

"If anything happens to him, I'll never forgive myself."

"Let's pray and ask God to heal him," Meg said.

"You pray. I'm not any good at it. God doesn't hear my prayers."

They bowed their heads and held hands while Meg asked for the healing power of God to reach down and touch that little life. She prayed for Allison and asked God to help her in whatever problems she had.

"Thank you for praying for Corley and for me," Allison said.

"I noticed your wedding band. Shouldn't we notify your husband?"

Allison looked down at her ring and began twisting it. Tears were back in her eyes as she said in an almost inaudible voice, "He was killed in Vietnam. I haven't wanted to take my ring off. It would be so final if I did."

Hearing about a death in Vietnam always struck terror in Meg's heart. Mike, her oldest son, was nineteen and in college, but he could be drafted anytime. He had wanted to join the Marines when he graduated from high school, but they had talked him into going to college first. Now his attitude was changing, and he was not so sure that the war was right.

"Would you like for me to call Sylvia's parents to be here with you?" Meg asked. "I think after the first shock, they'll accept you and Corley."

"No! Not now!" she replied nervously. "I can't handle rejection at this time. Maybe later."

The redheaded orderly brought a cot into the room for Allison to rest on. She insisted that she couldn't possibly sleep.

He looked at her kindly and said, "You look as if you could use some sleep, ma'am."

After the orderly left, Allison stretched out on the cot and was asleep as soon as her head touched the pillow.

Meg stayed all night. At ten she called home to make sure all was well there. A nurse brought her a cup of coffee around eleven, which helped keep her awake for a while. Toward morning, she dozed in the comfortable lounge chair. All through the night the nurses came in and out, changing intravenous bottles, adding antibiotics, and checking on the oxygen. They took Corley's temperature and gave him water while they were there.

Early the next morning, Dr. Gregory came in to see Corley. Allison was still sleeping, and Meg didn't wake her. The baby's breathing had improved, and the doctor was pleased with his progress. Meg followed him out of the room to have a private word with him.

"Doug, I'm ashamed of you. How could you be so rough on Allison? She has evidently been under a terrible strain and is a nervous wreck."

"She shouldn't have neglected that child, no matter what her personal problems are," he replied.

"Well, I think you owe her an apology," she said and flounced off.

Meg went to the cafeteria for coffee, and when she returned Dr. Newberry was at the desk looking at Corley's chart. His hair and beard had turned white early, but now his age had caught up and he had slowed down. However, he gave her his usual cheery greeting.

"Dr. Newberry," she said, "I want you to take over the care of my friend's little boy. You were the one I wanted, but you were out delivering a baby."

"Meg, Dr. Gregory is giving him the correct treatment, and there is no reason for me to take over."

"He was rude to my friend and I would rather have you."

"I'll speak to him, but let him continue to care for the baby. He's a capable young doctor, and I have all the practice I can handle."

"Okay, but he owes her an apology."

When Meg got back to the room, Allison was leaning over the crib looking at Corley. He was awake and smiling sleepily at her.

"He's so much better. I can't believe I slept so well. The past two nights I didn't sleep much, and I was worn out." She took the foam cup from Meg and said, "Thanks for the coffee."

"I'll stay with Corley while you go to the cafeteria and eat breakfast," Meg offered.

"First, I need to clean up and change clothes. I'm glad you brought my suitcases."

*****

In the cafeteria Allison started through the line and when she saw the food, she realized how hungry she was. She selected bacon, scrambled eggs, toast, orange juice, and coffee. While she ate, she felt someone standing over her and looked up into the smiling green eyes of the redheaded orderly.

"May I share your table?" he asked. "My name's Nick Nichols."

"Please sit down, Nick," she said. "Thank you for that cot. I slept well all night. I didn't realize I was so tired."

Nick set his tray on the table and sat across from her.

"You looked beat. Dr. Gregory ordered the cot."

"He did?" Allison asked in surprise. This was a new side of the doctor. She had felt that he didn't think about her as a person with needs. Only as a neglectful mother.

"Yeah, he's strict in the care of his patients, but on the whole he's a considerate man."

"He seems to be a good doctor. Corley is so much better. But he got on my case for not taking him sooner to get treatment, and he was right."

"What about your husband? Didn't he come with you?"

Allison glanced down at her ring and said softly, "He was killed in Vietnam."

"I'm sorry," he said and hurriedly changed the subject.

*****

Later, when Allison returned from the cafeteria, Meg drove home and went to bed. She slept until the children came home from school. They were full of questions about the sick baby and his mother.

"Who is she, and why haven't we met her?" demanded thirteen-year-old Sammy. He was named after his granddad, Sam Mitchell, and had his direct way of thinking and speaking. Physically, with black hair, tan skin, and contrasting light gray eyes, he was the most like his father of all the children.

"When the baby gets well is he going to stay with us?" asked Callie. She was eleven and the youngest of the family. She loved babies and frequently asked her parents to get her one. Jimmy, who was four years older than her, had always assured her that they didn't need any more babies. He was the middle child and sometimes felt left out.

"Yes, they'll visit us for awhile," Meg answered.

"Where are they going to sleep?" asked the practical Sarah. Almost seventeen, she had the fairest skin of all the children and, with her mother's brown hair and dark blue eyes, was her father's favorite.

"They'll stay in Callie's room, and she'll move in with you," Meg replied.

"That's not fair!" Sarah exclaimed. "Why can't the boys double up?"

"Sarah, I'm ashamed of you. When Mike is home from college, they always double up," Meg said.

"Dinner ready?" Joe asked as he came in the door from the garage. He put his arms around Meg. Nuzzling her neck, he said, "I missed you last night. My bed felt empty."

"Really, Daddy!" Sarah said. "You could wait until you're alone for that silly talk."

"You're home early," Meg said. "I haven't started dinner."

"I dismissed baseball practice for today so I could take my lovely family out for hamburgers at the Frosty Queen. Might even treat you to ice-cream for dessert."

"Oh, boy, can we have French fries, too?" Sammy asked.

"Sure," Joe said. "What are hamburgers without French fries?"

"I take it you stayed home and ate leftovers last night?" Meg said.

"Yeahhh!" they all agreed in unison.

After they had eaten and were home again, Joe said, "I'd like to go to the hospital with you and meet the beautiful, mysterious Allison. You are coming home tonight, aren't you?"

"Yes, I think Corley is a little better," she said. "I'll come home and sleep tonight, and then go to the hospital tomorrow afternoon and let Allison get out for some fresh air."

On the way to the hospital, she said, "Allison is so evasive that I think she's hiding something. She seems frightened. I wish she would confide in me."

When they entered the hospital room, they found Allison depressed and worn out. Corley was in her lap. His cheeks were wet with tears as he whimpered and squirmed around. The intravenous fluid, hanging on a pole, was still dripping through the needle in his hand. Tears came to Allison's eyes when she saw Meg and Joe.

"His temperature is back up and he cries when he's in his crib. They said he could be out of the tent for a little while, but he's so unhappy that I don't know what to do for him."

Meg took the baby from her and, holding him close, walked up and down the room, dragging the intravenous pole with her. "This is my husband Joe," she said. "We came to relieve you. Have you eaten supper?"

"No, and I couldn't eat a bite."

Joe took Allison by the arm and said, "I'll go to the cafeteria with you. I'd like a cup of coffee and a piece of pie. My wife wouldn't fix me any supper and made me take them out to the drive-in to eat."

As he was speaking, he led her out of the room. Meg could hear him talking to her all the way down the hall. She shook her head and grinned.

A nurse came in and gave Corley medicine by dropper and a glass of water. He drank the water greedily and then cuddled down on Meg's lap.

"This will lower his temperature and help him rest," the nurse told Meg.

When Corley dropped off to sleep, Meg placed him within the oxygen tent in his bed and sat back down in the rocker.

She puzzled over Allison's reaction when she had mentioned getting in touch with the Ashleys. It was as if she was afraid for them to know she was here. Meg had been surprised that Allison hadn't called her before she came. She didn't seem to be the type to barge in on people without letting them know ahead of time. Evidently she left in a hurry. Something had badly frightened her before she came. "I wonder what your mother is afraid of," she said to the sleeping baby.

Two hours later Joe and Allison came back. Allison was laughing and looked relaxed.

"We didn't care for this hospital food, so we went out to the Black Cat Café," Joe said. "The pie and coffee are much better there."

"This man made me walk and run in the park," Allison said with a laugh. "He said he didn't get to exercise his baseball team today so he would substitute me for them."

"You look as if it did you a world of good," Meg said.

"Thank you for staying with Corley. He looks as if he might sleep all night."

"The nurse gave him some medicine for his fever, and he went to sleep and has hardly moved," Meg replied. "I teach music at the schools two days a week, and tomorrow is one of my days, but I'll be here in the afternoon."

On the way home she discussed her concern over Allison's apparent troubles.

Joe agreed, but said, "She'll probably confide in us when she knows us better. You must remember, we're practically strangers to her."

Chapter III

The next afternoon when Meg reached the hospital, the first person she saw in the lobby was Mrs. Ashley.

"Why, Mrs. Ashley! What are you doing here?" she asked.

"Arlan has been having a little heart problem, and he's in for some tests," she said. "Is someone in your family ill?"

"No," Meg said hesitantly. "The daughter of an old friend of mine came to see us, and her little two-year-old son is very ill with pneumonia."

"Oh, the poor little thing. Who is your friend? Do I know her?"

"I knew her in Oklahoma City when I was working there during the war," Meg said evasively.

"I hope he gets well soon. It's a shame innocent little babies have to get sick. What floor is he on?"

"Second floor."

"That's the floor Arlan is on. When the little tyke gets better, we would like to meet him and his mother."

Allison was sitting in the rocker, holding Corley in her lap and feeding him oatmeal when Meg came in.

"Nick took the oxygen tent away because he's so much better. Dr. Gregory said that tomorrow they might take this intravenous out and give his antibiotics by mouth," she said happily.

Corley smiled at Meg from an oatmeal-covered face and said, "Hi."

"Well, hello," she said. "You feel like talking today, don't you?"

"Dr. Gregory was almost human today," Allison said. "He's pleased with Corley's progress."

Meg noticed that Allison looked better also. She still wore her hair in a pony-tail and had on clean jeans and a plaid shirt, but the worry lines that had etched her face were gone.

"Allison, I want to tell you something before you find out on your

26

own and are surprised. I met your grandmother, Mrs. Ashley, in the lobby. Your grandfather is a patient in this hospital, and is on this very floor. Would you like to meet them?"

"No! Not now. Maybe later. How will you explain my presence here?" she asked.

"I told her that you were the daughter of a friend I knew in Oklahoma City, which wasn't exactly a lie. We shared an apartment there with another friend, Sue Gregory, after we graduated from high school. Sue is Dr. Gregory's older sister."

"Did...did you know my father?"

"Yes, I knew him," Meg replied. "You resemble him. He was in the Air Force and was tall and handsome, with black hair and brown eyes. Sylvia loved him very much. It was a wartime romance."

"He must have been one of those love-'em-and-leave-'em types," she said with a sigh.

Meg mentally agreed, but was silent.

After a pause Allison asked, "What's his name?"

"John Hook."

They visited awhile and then Allison said, "While you're here, I think I'll go to the cafeteria and grab a bite."

"Good idea," Meg nodded

It was still early, so not too many people were there. While Allison stood in line choosing her food, Nick came up behind her and said, "Hello, again. I see you're eating early, too. May I join you?"

"Sure, I'm glad to have company."

After they sat down Allison asked, "Is Nick your real first name?"

"Believe it or not it's Nicholas Nichols. Isn't that awful? My father's first name was Robert, but all of his life he was called Nick. When I was born he said, 'He'll always go by Nick, so we might as well name him that.'"

"Didn't two Nicks in the family get confusing?"

Nick leaned forward, made a funny face and said, "Don't tell anyone but they called me 'Nicky' until I got old enough to object."

As Allison laughed at him, she glanced up and met the eyes of Dr. Gregory. He had just come through the door with another doctor.

The two doctors bought coffee and sandwiches and sat at a table across the room from them.

Nick kept Allison amused throughout the meal. Out of the corner of her eye, she could see Dr. Gregory glance at them occasionally. She wondered if the solemn man ever laughed.

*****

Allison hadn't been gone long when Mrs. Ashley poked her head in the door of Corley's room and asked, "May I come in and meet the little boy?"

"Sure," Meg replied. "He's awake and feeling better."

Corley was sitting in the crib playing with a set of keys that Meg had given him. He looked up at Mrs. Ashley and smiled.

"What an adorable child," she said. "I love babies. Wish Sylvia could have had a houseful. Arlan and I wanted more children, but the Lord didn't see fit to give them to us."

Mrs. Ashley visited awhile with Meg and Corley, but she was gone by the time Allison returned.

*****

The next day was Saturday and Joe accompanied Meg to the hospital. When they walked into Corley's room, both the Ashleys were there. Mr. Ashley, in pajamas and robe, was sitting in the lounge chair holding him on his lap. Corley was laughing and hugging a teddy bear that the Ashleys had purchased in the gift shop.

"It looks as if you've found a grandson," Joe commented.

"I wish he were," Mrs. Ashley said, looking fondly at him. "He's so precious. Your parents and grandparents must be proud of him."

"Yes they are," Allison agreed.

Meg thought it was a good time to tell them the truth, but Allison made no move to do so.

"How are your tests coming?" Joe asked Mr. Ashley.

"Everything is okay," he said. "I have to watch my diet and exercise."

"He gets enough exercise in the store," Mrs. Ashley said. "What he needs is more fresh air and relaxation."

"Thank you for your diagnosis, Dr. Ella," her husband said with a laugh.

Chapter IV

Two days later, Corley was sitting on a rug on the floor of his hospital room, playing with a truck that the Ashleys had brought him when Dr. Gregory walked in.

Rising from the chair where she sat reading a magazine, Allison said, "Hello, Dr. Gregory. I think Corley is a lot better."

"Yes, he's responding well to treatment," the doctor said.

Corley looked up and grinned at him and said, "Hi."

"Hi, yourself, Corley," he said and bent down to tousle his hair. "I believe you're just about cured. Get back in bed and let me listen to your chest."

Corley smiled at him, obediently climbed up into his crib, and pulled up his pyjama top.

Dr. Gregory warmed his stethoscope in the palm of his hand for a minute before placing it on Corley's chest. "Sounds good. Want to listen?"

Corley nodded his head and then listened intently after Dr. Gregory placed the earpieces in his ears. A grin spread on his face. "Boom, boom," he said.

"That's right, a good boom, boom," the doctor said. "Now let me look in your mouth."

Corley obediently opened his mouth, stuck out his little pink tongue, and said, "Ahhhh."

"Looks great, now the ears." Corley turned one side of his head to the doctor, and then the other. "You sure do know the routine, Corley," Doctor Gregory said.

Putting his otoscope away, he turned to Allison, and said, "You may take him home today. I'll give you some prescriptions, and you're to follow the directions on them exactly. Do you understand?"

"Of course I do. You don't think much of my ability, do you?"

"Sorry. I shouldn't be so blunt. Corley appears to have received

29

good care, which helped him recover quickly. I don't understand your neglect of his well-being in this last illness."

Allison looked away and didn't answer.

"Bring him to my office in a week. Will you be staying with the Sullivans?"

"Yes, for the time being," she answered.

After he left she went to the pay phone, called Meg, and told her the good news.

"I'll be there as soon as I can," Meg said.

Nick came by to see them before they left. He had visited them occasionally when he could spare a few moments from his work. Whenever he took his meal breaks he would stop by to see if she was ready to eat. She went with him and enjoyed his company.

She found out from one of the nurses that Nick had been a medic in the army and had served a year in Vietnam. "That's the reason he's able to do so many technical things the other orderlies can't do," she said. "Don't mention Vietnam to him, though. He doesn't want to talk about it."

Knowing Nick had served in Vietnam caused Allison to feel closer to him. She wished she could talk to him about it and find out more what it was like for Brad.

"Hi, Corley," Nick said. "You're looking great."

Corley grinned at him and said, "Hi, Nick!"

Nick turned to Allison and said, "I hear you're leaving today. I'm going to miss you both. Where will you be staying?"

"We'll be with friends in Oak Grove."

"Could I drop by sometime? I'd like to see how Corley is doing."

"I'd like that, but I'm not sure of my plans yet."

*****

A half an hour later Meg arrived and Corley was checked out of the hospital. Nick insisted on carrying their suitcases to the station-wagon.

"Nick seems like a nice, caring man," Meg said when they were on their way. "He's very polite, also."

"Yes, He's been good to Corley and me," Allison replied.

"I think you made quite an impression on him," Meg said with a smile.

The drive on a winding road through wooded hills was lovely. Occasionally they crossed wooden bridges that spanned the frothy rapids of small creeks. When they reached Oak Grove, they stopped at Glass Drug Store to get the prescriptions filled.

"While we're waiting on the prescriptions, let's get a cherry Coke," Meg said. "When we were in high school, your mother and I, along with our friends Amy and Sue, came in here lots of times for cherry Cokes or ice-cream sodas. It was a hang-out for teenagers. Now that so many cars are available to them, the Freezer Queen drive-in is the place where the teens go."

Allison was delighted with the interior of the drugstore. It still had an old-fashioned marble counter and marble-top tables along with the wire-back chairs.

"The store hasn't changed much, except the older Mr. Glass is gone, and his son has taken his place," Meg explained.

She bought cherry Cokes for Allison and herself, and a grape soda for Corley.

While they drank the Cokes, Allison asked, "Sometime will you show me pictures of my mother and the rest of her friends?"

"Sure, I'd like to see them again myself. Meeting you, Sylvia's daughter, brings back old memories. Several of us were in here on Sunday afternoon, December 7, 1941, when Mr. Glass came out of his office all excited over the news that Pearl Harbor had been attacked by the Japanese. Most of us didn't even know where Pearl Harbor was located, or why it was important to the United States. We soon learned, though. It was the end of innocence for our country. Even this sleepy little town changed when fathers, brothers, and sons departed for the armed forces. Others left to work in war plants." When they came out of the drugstore, Meg pointed to a large store nearby with "Ashley's Grocery Store" across the front over the door.

"Your grandparents' store," she said. "Down there at the end of the block is my dad's hardware store."

Allison glanced up and down the street and noticed that the business part of town was only two blocks long. At the end of Main Street she saw a white stone church with a steeple.

"What a pretty church," Allison said. "Is that where you attend?"

"That's the Methodist church where your mother attended. We go to the Baptist church. It's on past that one."

"Are you sure you have room for us?" Allison asked. "Is there a motel where we could stay?"

"We have plenty of room and I won't hear of you going to a motel."

Allison was relieved. She would feel safer with a family than alone in a motel room.

Two miles out of town, Meg turned up the winding road to her house on Blueberry Hill. Allison had been too worried and exhausted to notice the house before. It was a large, rambling ranch style, made of native stone, with a shingled roof and attached garage. The glass windows across the front of the house offered a view of the river and hills beyond. From the attached garage, they passed through a huge sunny kitchen into a hall. Four large bedrooms and two baths opened off this passageway. Meg left Allison to unpack her suitcases in one of the bedrooms while she went back to the kitchen to make iced tea. When Allison finished putting her clothes away, she came into the kitchen.

"Your house is lovely," she said.

"Thank you. Would you like to see the rest of it?"

"I'd love to," she answered.

Corley trailed after them as Meg led them into the combination living and dining room. The glass windows extending across the front of the house let in plenty of light, as well as offering a beautiful view of the river. Beyond the river, the undulating hills swept off in the distance.

A large stone fireplace filled one end of the living area. Another door opened off the dining area into a hall between that area and the kitchen. A stairway in the hall led to the master bedroom. Meg took Alison up to see the room. It was situated over the living-dining area. A long dormer window faced the river, and a large closet and a bathroom with a skylight were on the opposite side.

"This is a beautiful house," Allison said.

"Thank you. Joe and I designed it, and he built most of it by himself. Our friend, Mel Bradford, who owns the lumber company did some of the work, and I helped a little."

Soon the children came home from school and were excited to find Allison and Corley there. They went to their rooms and each brought back a toy purchased from their allowances for the little boy. Corley immediately sat down on the floor to play, and Allison said, "What do you say, Corley?"

He looked up and smiled at them and said, "T'ank you."

"You're welcome," they chorused, and sat down on the floor to play with him.

"I noticed my car has been washed and the inside cleaned. Who did that?" Allison asked.

"Jimmy and I did it," Sammy said.

"It was nice of you and looks like a good job well done."

"Sarah and I washed your clothes," Callie said shyly.

"Well, I thank you for that," she said and smiled at her.

Surrounded by the children and toys, Corley smiled and laughed. Even Sarah was captivated by him and declared him the sweetest and best baby in the world.

Allison helped Meg prepare supper while the children kept Corley entertained. When Joe and Jimmy came home from baseball practice, they were happy to see the visitors. Joe tossed Corley up in the air, as he had done all of his children when they were small, and Corley laughed gleefully.

"Don't be too rough with him, Joe," Meg said. "He hasn't completely recovered."

After supper, Joe and the boys went down to the basement and brought up the old crib and mattress, and set it up in Callie's bedroom. Sarah changed the sheets on the bed, and Callie moved her clothes and other possessions into Sarah's room.

"I'm afraid I'm putting you girls out, taking one of your bedrooms this way," Allison said.

"Oh, no. We don't mind," Sarah replied.

"We're glad to have you and Corley stay with us," Callie agreed.

In bed that night, listening to the soft breathing of Corley, Allison thought over the events of the day. She was a little bit mollified because Dr. Gregory had said that Corley appeared to be well taken care of. The doctor was handsome! All the nurses rushed to help him when he needed something. Maybe that was the kind of treatment he expected from everyone. Well, she for one wasn't going to fall at his feet!

The Sullivans were so nice to her, and they made her feel welcome. Joe and Meg seemed to be very much in love. "Maggie" he called her. No one else called her by that name. It made it something special between them.

Eventually she relaxed and dozed off. Suddenly she saw the face of the murderer. He held a gun in his hand. It was pointed at her! She awoke with a start. It was only a dream, but the memory of the murder came back into her mind. Reliving the horror of the terrible event, she became apprehensive. She had let the police know that she had witnessed the crime, and there was someone in the department who must be in the pay of the murderers. Now she was afraid that somehow they would find her.

"Don't be silly," she told herself, "How could they find me? I didn't give them my name." Still, she had an icy feeling in the pit of her stomach when she thought of it. She could still see the cold, hard face of the killer. That was the reason she didn't want to let the Ashleys know who she was. It might put them in danger.

She didn't want anyone else killed.

Chapter V

On the day Allison fled Chicago, Detective Gil MacDonald was back in the station after visiting the parking garage where the body of a man had been found. He had been shot in the middle of the forehead, gangland style. Several people were questioned, but no one had witnessed the murder. The body had been taken to the morgue for identification and autopsy.

The phone on his desk jangled. He picked it up and said, "MacDonald here."

It was Captain Schumaker. "Mac," he said, "we have an identification on the body found in the garage. He was an undercover cop named Tony Patrino. He was investigating the Giovanni gang."

Mac rubbed his hand over his thinning brown hair. "This is serious. I'll find Dom Giovanni and have a talk with him. I'm sure he'll have all kinds of witnesses as to his whereabouts during the time of the murder."

After he replaced the receiver, the phone rang again and the switchboard operator said, "We just received a call from some woman who said she had witnessed a murder in a parking garage, but she didn't give her name and hung up before we could question her. She did give us a license number, and we're checking it out."

"Let me know as soon as you get it," he said.

"What's up, boss?" Danny Webb asked. He was a young rookie cop who was serving apprenticeship in the office.

"Murder of an undercover cop in a parking garage. A witness just called and gave us a license number, but neglected to give her name," he replied.

Detective Chuck Brogan, who had been sitting at his desk filling out reports, rose and stretched. "I'm going out for some fresh air," he said. "Can't stand being cooped up here all day."

"On your way back, get me a hot dog from one of those vendors out front," Dirk Vance said from his desk in the corner.

"Aren't you supposed to be losing weight?" Mac asked.

"I am, I am," he replied. "But I can't go cold turkey. Have them put on onions and mustard, no relish. That ought to be less fattening."

"Okay," Chuck said and sauntered out the door with his hands in his pockets.

As soon as he got outside he turned the next corner and hurried down the block to Casey's Bar. After he made sure no other policemen were there, he headed to the rest rooms, but stopped at the phone booth in the hall and made a call.

When he came back to the station, he had two hot dogs. The plain one for Dirk, and one with chili for himself.

"Now why did you get one with chili when you know I can't have it?" Dirk asked.

"I didn't get it for you," Chuck said, handing him the plain one and taking a huge bite out of the other one.

"You like to torture a guy, don't you?" Dirk grumbled.

Mac was on the phone, and when he hung up, he turned and said, "Guess what. Dom Giovanni just reported his Lincoln was stolen, and the license plates just happen to match the ones on the car that was seen at the garage after the murder. We're bringing him in for questioning anyway. I'm going to the garage and question the attendant again."

The attendant, Harry Brown, was a blond young man with blue eyes and a slight case of acne. He was still puffed up with importance about the discovery of the body in the garage. Television and other news media had been there taking pictures and questioning him about the murder.

"Harry," Mac said, "you said three or four cars left the garage within the half hour before the body was discovered, but you didn't know any of them. Is that right?"

"Yeah."

"Were any of them women?"

"Only one, and boy, was she a looker!"

"Can you describe her?"

"She had sorta long, black hair and brown eyes."

"What was her demeanor?"

Harry looked at him blankly and said, "Huh?"

"Was she nervous or scared looking?"

"Now that you mention it, she did look a little queer, and she seemed to be in a big hurry."

"Did you see which building she had been in?"

"Sure. I saw her when she parked her car. Couldn't help but notice her, you know. She went into the office building right next door."

"Is there someone who can relieve you so you can come to the station and help our artist draw her likeness?"

"Sure, my relief is here now," he said as another young man approached them.

"Buddy," he said importantly, "I need to go to the police station to help them on this murder case. Not sure when I'll be back."

After an hour of working together, Harry and the police artist produced a picture that resembled Allison.

"That's her!" shouted Harry gleefully. "Boy, you know your business!"

Copies were run off and Mac took them to the building next to the garage. He showed them to the security guards and asked, "Did you see this young lady earlier today?"

They studied the picture and one of them said, "Sure, I saw her. She took the elevator, but I didn't see her after that."

A young man passing them glanced curiously at the picture in the policeman's hand and said, "Oh, that's a picture of the beautiful woman that was here earlier today."

"Did you see where she went?"

"Yeah, she was going into the law offices of Connel and Estes around one p.m. I'm sure of the time, because I was returning from my lunch break," he said.

Mac went to the lawyers' offices to find out her identity, but they wouldn't help him.

"We can't divulge our clients or their business," Mr. Estes said. "There must be some reason that the caller didn't reveal her name. Do you know what it could have been?"

Two days later, Mac sat at his desk thinking about the case. At first he thought the woman just didn't want to get involved, but maybe there was another reason. It was strange that Dom Giovanni would report his car stolen immediately after they learned the license number of the killers' car. Even odder was the fact that it turned out to be his! He glanced around the office. Could one of his co-workers be on Giovanni's payroll? It was hard to believe, but he knew that some policemen did go on the take.

There were only the four of them here when the call came about the car license. The rookie, Danny Webb, Dirk Vance, and Chuck Brogan. He paused in his cogitating. Chuck Brogan was the only one who had left the room. It could be him! Recently he had been demoted and given a desk job because of his rough treatment of prisoners. He had constantly griped about this until Mac told him to shut up or get out.

He ran his hand over his hair and quietly got up. The others were busy at their desks. Only Danny looked up questioningly. "Be back in a minute," he told him.

The closest phone outside the station was around the corner at Casey's Bar. He entered and saw the bartender Hank wiping a wet rag around on the bar. Not many customers frequented the place at this time of day.

"Hi, Lieutenant," he grinned at him. "What'll you have?"

"Just a Coke," he said.

After Hank had opened the Coke and placed it with a glass in front of him, Mac asked, "Do you remember if Sgt. Chuck Brogan came in around four on Monday afternoon?"

Hank thought for a minute, and then replied.

"Sure. I remember. He only came in to use the rest room. Was yours stopped up or something?"

"Not to my knowledge. He didn't even buy a beer?"

"No. He only used the rest room and the phone."

Mac finished his Coke, wiped his mouth on a napkin, put a dollar on the bar, and left. When he got back to the station, he went past the squad room and knocked on Captain Schumaker's door.

"Come in," the captain said. "Have a chair."

Mac sat down and said, "Captain, I wonder if we have a mole in our office. Why else would Dom Giovanni report his car stolen minutes after we found it had been seen at the murder site? Who would have the nerve to steal a well-known Mafia boss's car anyway?"

"I've been thinking the same thing. Do you have a suspect?"

"Chuck Brogan was there when I got the call, and he's the only one who left the room afterward. I found out he went to Casey's Bar and used the phone at that time."

"He doesn't like the desk job we gave him after he nearly killed that kid he caught stealing," the captain said. "It wasn't the first time that he badly roughed up a suspect, either. I can't tolerate that kind of policeman. A little authority goes to his head, and he abuses those over whom he has power."

"A person like that is dangerous. He could do anything to get even if he feels like he's been put down," Mac said. "He may be in Dom Giovanni's pay, and that woman could have heard them mention that they had a spy in the police station."

"You may be right," the captain said. "I'll put a tail on him. He's an angry person and could very well be venting his spite by working for the Mafia. I hope not, though, for his sake as well as ours. Also for that woman who witnessed the crime. Ned Sutton is the hired gun for the Giovanni family.

"And he's a force to be reckoned with."

Chapter VI

On Sunday morning Allison and Corley went to the Baptist church with the Sullivan family. The sun, shining brightly through the trees surrounding the church, cast leafy shadows on the plain, white frame building with the clear glass windows. It was a new experience for Allison because it was so different from the large brick church with the stained glass windows that she had attended in Evanston.

As they pulled into the parking-lot, other families emerged from their cars and called friendly greetings to each other as they herded their children into the Sunday School wing. The Sullivan children quickly exited the station-wagon to join their friends. When Meg and Allison took Corley to the nursery, he walked in and made a beeline for the building blocks in a corner.

"I don't think we'll have a problem with him," the teacher said with a laugh.

"'Bye, Corley," Allison said.

Corley turned away briefly from the blocks, grinned at her, waved a chubby little hand, and said, "Bye-bye."

Meg taught the younger women, so Allison went with her to class. She enjoyed the lesson and the association with the other women. Most were also mothers of young children, and she felt a kinship with them.

When the class was over, Meg and Allison went by the nursery to check on Corley. They looked through a small glass window in the door and saw Corley sitting on a little chair in a semicircle with three other children listening to the teacher tell a Bible story.

Outside the church building, they met Meg's father Sam Mitchell and stepmother Alice. Sam was in his late sixties, of medium height with a compact build, gray hair, and friendly gray eyes. Alice, in her fifties, had brown hair streaked with gray, soft brown eyes, and a timid manner. Meg had told Allison that they had a son named Luke who was a month younger than her oldest son Mike. The boys were best friends and attended the University of Oklahoma in Norman.

Meg left to sing in the choir, the children went in with their friends, and Joe escorted Allison into the auditorium.

Allison looked around curiously. The interior of the building was as plain as the outside. A blue carpet covered the floor, the windows were unadorned glass, the wooden pews were cushion-less, and a plain wooden cross hung over the baptistery. On the communion table in front of the pulpit was a bouquet of spring flowers.

"Will we see the Ashleys?" she whispered to Joe.

"No, they go to the Methodist church," he replied.

When the choir filed in, Allison was surprised to see Dr. Gregory there. He smiled at her, and she was glad she was wearing her stylish green suit with a gold necklace and matching gold earrings.

The pastor, Brother Mark Lyons, was a young man not long out of the seminary. Allison had met his wife Donna in Sunday School and had learned that they had a ten-month-old son named Joshua.

Before the sermon Meg sang a solo, "His Eye is on the Sparrow," and Allison was impressed with her beautiful voice.

After the service, many people came up to meet her and welcome her to their church and town. Among them were the Gregorys, the doctor's parents. Dr. Gregory resembled his father who was tall with gray eyes and gray hair. His mother was short and plump with brown eyes and only a little gray in her black curly hair.

On the way home Allison said, "You have a lovely soprano voice, Meg. I was enthralled with your singing."

"That's why I married her," Joe said. "I fell in love with her voice first."

"Aren't you ever serious, Joe?" Allison asked with a laugh.

"I try not to be," he said with a twinkle in his eye.

After dinner, Meg asked Allison if she would like to see Sylvia's grave.

"Yes, and could we take flowers?" she asked.

While Corley took a nap, Allison accompanied Meg outside to her garden to cut some flowers. Roses were Meg's favorite, and she had several bushes of different varieties and colors.

"Which ones would you like to take for your mother's grave?" Meg asked.

"They're all so beautiful," Allison said. "But, I like this shade of red best."

"Take this pair of scissors and cut several," Meg said. "My mother's favorite color was pink, so I'll take these. I'm also cutting some for other friends."

By the time they finished, Corley was awake. Allison dressed him and then let him help her carry the basket of roses to the station-wagon while Meg followed with a jar of water.

Allison tried to hold back the tears when she saw her birth mother's grave. Her mother had been only eighteen when she became pregnant. Several years younger than she, Allison, was now. Since she didn't want to embarrass her parents she had gone by herself to a strange town to have her baby. How frightened she must have been. To go through the ordeal of birth alone, without friends or family, and then to give up her baby.

She was a brave, conscientious person. Allison was proud of her. Even though she hadn't known her, she felt love for her. She regretted that she didn't look for her sooner and get acquainted with her.

The grave was still fairly new, and the mound of dirt had not settled completely. The headstone was in place, and she read:

Sylvia Ashley Bachman
b. April 25, 1926
d. March 22, 1970
Beloved wife and daughter

"I wish I could have known her," Allison said as she brushed a tear from her eye.

After they placed the flowers in the urns on either side of the marker, they turned and saw Mrs. Ashley approaching.

"Meg, it's so good of you to remember Sylvia with flowers!" she exclaimed. "Those beautiful roses were Sylvia's favorite shade of red."

"I'm glad to do it. I have flowers for my mother's grave, and also some for Tommy's and Jimmy's graves," Meg replied. "I told Allison they were all my good friends."

Tears came to Mrs. Ashley's eyes. "I wish we could go back to those dear days before the war, when you were all children and no one thought of death."

Corley had been examining a small stone lamb marker on a child's grave nearby, but when he saw Mrs. Ashley he came to them, looked up at her and said, "Hi!"

She stooped down and hugged him and said, "But then you wouldn't be here, would you? You are an adorable child."

They talked a few minutes longer and then left to go to Meg's mother's grave. Mrs. Ashley stood at Sylvia's graveside with bowed head in silent contemplation.

"It's so sad. How she must have loved Sylvia!" Allison said.

"Yes, both her parents thought the sun rose and set on her," Meg replied.

Allison had a pensive look on her face and said, "It's strange that Sylvia liked the same shade of red roses that I like."

When they reached her mother's grave, Meg placed roses in the vase on it. She told Allison that her mother had died when she lost control of her car while coming home from Wolfeton during a rainstorm.

In the veterans part of the cemetery, they placed roses on Tommy Riggs's grave.

"My friend Amy and he were married the day after we graduated from high school in 1944. He was a gunner on a B-24 and had already been on twenty-five bombing missions and was back in the States, stationed in Florida. Shortly after their marriage, his crew was sent back to Europe and their plane was shot down coming from a bombing mission. There were no survivors, but all of the bodies were recovered."

"I know how she felt," Allison said sadly. "All wars are the same for wives."

"And parents," Meg added. "After his death, Amy went into nurses' training at University Hospital in Oklahoma City. Later my brother Bob was in medical school there, and they ran into each other, began dating and eventually married. Now they're medical missionaries in the Philippines."

"I'm glad she was able to find someone else," Allison said.

As they placed roses on Jimmy's grave, Meg told her that she had known him all of her life and that they had frequently sung together in school and church.

"Before he left for the service, he told me that he loved me. I liked him a lot but didn't feel that kind of love for him. Even then Joe was the only one for me. We named our second son, James Lester, after him. Our Jimmy is as sweet and gentle as the one for whom he was named."

Chapter VII

Allison was surprised when the children dressed in jeans, tee shirts, and tennis shoes without socks to go to school Monday morning. She hadn't noticed their clothes when she came home from the hospital with Corley.

Meg saw the expression on her face. She laughed and said, "That's the latest style in school for boys and girls. We don't care much for it, but kids have to dress like their peers. Makes buying and washing clothes simpler. Long hair for both boys and girls is also the mode. Joe likes it on the girls, but won't tolerate it on the boys, except Mike. In college Mike is sort of out of his reach."

The telephone rang, and Meg answered it. When she came back in the kitchen she said, "That was Mary Lou Vandenberg. You met her yesterday at church. She was reminding me that softball practice for the girls starts this afternoon. We're going to coach the older girls' team. Her daughters, Kathy and Mandy, and our Sarah will be on it. Callie will be on the grade school team. Would you and Corley like to go with us?"

"Sure, I played softball when I was younger."

"Maybe you could help coach."

Allison helped Meg wash the dishes and clean the house during the morning and, after a light lunch, she put Corley down for his nap.

"Meg, I need to buy some more socks and underwear for Corley. Is it okay with you if I go to town while he sleeps?" Allison asked.

"Sure, go ahead. I'll watch him."

Allison changed into a clean pair of jeans and a cotton shirt and drove her car to town. She parked and went into the Dixie Emporium. When she came out with her purchases, she heard the honking of a car. She glanced up and saw a van pull into the parking space near her. A grinning redheaded man climbed out. It was the hospital orderly, Nick.

"Of all the good luck meeting you here!" he said.

"What are you doing in Oak Grove?" she asked.

"I brought a patient home in this hospital van," he explained. "The hospital figures it's cheaper than an ambulance when a patient only needs a ride. How 'bout going for a cup of coffee with me?"

"Okay, but I have to be at the Sullivan's by 3:30. I'm going to help coach the girls softball team."

Over coffee he asked about Corley. She told him Corley felt better and enjoyed the attention he received from the Sullivan children. Then she asked about the hospital.

"It isn't the same without you and Corley there," he said. "I miss our meals together."

"Oh, I imagine you find plenty of nurses to eat with," she said with a laugh.

He grinned, shrugged his shoulders, and said, "Maybe a few."

"You're such a clown. I suspect you're quite a ladies' man."

"Speaking of clowns, there's a small circus coming to Wolfeton next week. Would you and Corley like to go?"

"Oh, yes! I love circuses and I know Corley will be thrilled. He's never been to one."

"The opening day is Thursday and I'm off that day. Is that day okay with you?"

"Sure. I don't have any plans for that week. If something comes up I'll call you at the hospital. Would you like for us to meet you in Wolfeton so you wouldn't have to come out of your way?"

"No. When I take a lady and her child on a date, I pick them up at their home. Just give me directions and I'll be there next Thursday at ten a.m. We'll go to the afternoon show but get there early so we'll have the whole day for all of the festivities."

*****

When the children came home from school, Allison and Corley accompanied them to the ballpark. There were four diamonds, two for boys' baseball and two for girls' softball. The older boys weren't practicing yet, because most of them were on the high-school team and their season wasn't over. Sammy was on the younger boys' team.

Mary Lou Vandenberg was a short blonde woman in her early forties, with a heart-shaped face, sky-blue eyes, and a lively personality. Allison remembered her from church. Her husband Brock was the vice-president of the Oak Grove Bank, and his father Brock, Sr. was president. Kathy, the oldest of her two daughters, was a young replica of her mother, with naturally curly blonde hair and azure eyes, while Mandy had the straight brown hair and hazel eyes of her father. She was pretty, but was quiet and shy and didn't have the sparkle her sister had.

Before practice began, Jan, the coach for Callie's team, came over and said that she needed an assistant, so Allison agreed to help her. The girls took turns watching Corley. Callie always took him over with a proprietary air between her turns at bat or fielding.

*****

As she prepared for bed that night Allison thought about all of the happenings of the day. It was so strange meeting Nick in town. It couldn't have been planned because he had no idea that she'd be there. It was a coincidence, but what if she ran into one of the killers that way. She shuddered. They'll never find me, though, she told herself. Could they?

Yes, it was possible...

Chapter VIII

Tuesdays and Fridays were the days that Meg taught school. "I hate to leave you by yourself," she said on Tuesday morning.

"I'm a big girl," Allison replied with a smile. "This morning I intend to go to Ashleys' Grocery Store to buy applesauce for Corley. I noticed you were low on milk, so I'll pick up a gallon while I'm there. Is there anything else you need?"

"Don't do that. I plan to get groceries on my way home."

"I want to help with expenses. I feel like I'm imposing on you. Corley is better now. We need to find an apartment of our own."

"We love having you stay with us. If you want to help with the food, it will be okay. Here's a list of things we need."

Later in the store, Allison placed Corley in a cart and began searching for the items on Meg's grocery list. As she walked down an aisle looking for a certain brand of applesauce she heard Corley say, "Hi!" Looking up she saw Mrs. Ashley.

"Well, Hi yourself, little fellow," Mrs. Ashley said. "I'm glad to see you both. I intended to call you today, Allison. Could you and Corley come to our house for supper tonight? We'd love to have you."

"Thanks, we'll be glad to come," Allison responded.

When Meg came home and heard the news, she was delighted. "I hoped you'd get better acquainted," she said.

At six that evening, Allison rang the doorbell at the large white Ashley home. Mr. Ashley greeted them at the door, and Mrs. Ashley came out of the kitchen wiping her hands on her apron.

"Dinner is almost ready," she said. "Make yourselves comfortable here with Arlan."

"It smells good. May I help you?" Allison asked.

"Well, come on in. You can help put the food on the table."

Mr. Ashley led Corley into the living-room where a small red wagon awaited him. Corley immediately put his teddy bear in it and began pulling it around the room.

After the meal Allison insisted on helping with the dishes.

"Sylvia always helped me with dinner and the dishes when she was home," Mrs. Ashley reminisced as they worked together washing the dishes and cleaning the kitchen.

When they returned to the living-room they found Mr. Ashley pulling Corley in the wagon.

The room was full of photographs of Sylvia at all ages of her life. Allison noted the resemblance to Mrs. Ashley. The same narrow face, tilted nose, and small mouth. Only, instead of brown eyes, her eyes were gray like her father's. They were her finest feature. However, the similarity ended there, for he was a large florid man with graying, sandy hair.

Mrs. Ashley came up beside her as she looked at the pictures. "Sylvia was our only child and she was very dear to us. Having these pictures around makes her seem close." Tears gathered in her eyes as she added. "Sometimes I forget she's gone and think she'll call or walk in the door."

"That's the feeling I had after my husband was killed," Allison commented.

Mrs. Ashley reminisced further. "She wanted to come home to die, so her husband Bernard brought her here. He stayed with her to the end and was a great help and comfort to us. Meg came over and helped, also."

Allison hugged her. "She was a very lucky girl to have had parents who gave her so much love."

Mrs. Ashley wiped her eyes with a Kleenex. "Thank you. You're so kind and understanding. Although you have great beauty, you're modest and don't flaunt it. Your parents must have been exceptional."

Allison was embarrassed. "Yes, they were great. When I got a lot of attention as a child, my mother would talk to me about it later. 'Better to be beautiful on the inside than the outside,' she would say. She stressed kindness and politeness, and putting others first."

"That's a wonderful outlook," Mrs. Ashley said.

"Another thing she told me was that although you can't help how you look, you do have control over how you act."

"She is very wise," Mrs. Ashley said. "I would like to meet her."

"She passed away a few weeks ago," Allison said sadly.

"I'm so sorry. I've been so wrapped up in our loss that I didn't realize that you had suffered two great losses, your mother as well as your husband."

Mr. Ashley, who had been listening to their conversation, commented, "You're tall and pretty enough to be a model. Have you ever tried that?"

"Yes," Allison admitted. "When I was in college I did some modeling to help pay expenses."

At eight, Allison stated that she must go home and put Corley to bed. Corley wanted to take the wagon with him.

"No, Corley," Allison said. "You have enough toys at the Sullivan's house."

"You'll have it to play with when you come to visit us the next time," Mrs. Ashley explained. "You will come again, won't you, Allison?"

Allison sensed the loneliness in their lives. "Yes, anytime you invite us. Thanks for a lovely evening."

Chapter IX

That same Tuesday afternoon as Joe watched his baseball team practice, he became concerned about one of his players. Frankie Hunter was a newcomer to the school and team, and, although he was only a freshman, he had talent. He fielded the ball accurately, batted satisfactorily, and ran like a rabbit. Today, however, he was not doing well. His arm seemed weak, and his batting and running were not up to par.

Joe called him over to his side to see if he could discover the reason for his poor showing. When he placed his hand on Frankie's shoulder in a friendly manner, the boy winced with pain. Recovering quickly, he smiled at Joe, but Joe was suspicious.

"Wait in the dugout until practice is over. I want to talk to you in my office," he said.

Frankie walked slowly to the dugout, dragging his feet.

When practice ended and the equipment was put away, Joe told Jimmy to wait in the pickup, and then he took Frankie to his office.

Frankie looked scared, but Joe reassured him. "I just want to find out why you aren't doing as well as usual," he said. "Pull up your shirt."

"Do I hafta?" Frankie asked.

"Yes, unless you'd rather go see the principal."

Slowly Frankie lifted his shirt, and Joe was aghast at the red welts across his back.

"Who did that?" he asked in a tight voice.

"I-I fell against a ladder," the boy said.

"That won't wash. We both know how it happened. I just want to know who did it."

Frankie hung his head and said hesitantly, "M-my paw." Then he looked up, terrified, and added, "B-but he didn't mean to, and I deserved it. I was bad."

"Frankie, no one deserves that. I'm going to take you home and have a talk with your father."

"No, no, please don't," he begged. "It'll make him mad, and I did need it."

In spite of his protests, Joe led him to the pickup. "Move over, Jimmy," he said. "We're taking Frankie home."

Jimmy obediently scooted over, Frankie reluctantly climbed in beside him, and Joe shut the door.

Joe seethed with anger toward a father who would do this to his son. He remembered the many brutal beatings that he had received from his uncle when he was a boy. He had made a promise to God that if ever he saw that abuse to another child, he would do something about it. But now he needed to get hold of himself and do things God's way. As he drove, he silently prayed that the Lord would take away his anger and give him peace of mind and love to confront this man.

Frankie directed them out of town and up in the hills to a little-used road that was mostly a pair of ruts. It led to a run-down shack surrounded by three dilapidated sheds. A few chickens were enclosed in a pen, and a man in overalls was coming from the cowshed with a bucket of milk. He paused briefly when he saw them, but he took the milk into the house and then came back outside. Two little girls, swinging on a tire tied to a rope slung over a tree branch, stopped and stared.

Joe and the two boys climbed out of the pickup, and Frankie approached his father with trepidation.

"Paw, this is my coach, Mr. Sullivan," he said. "He wants to meetcha."

"Hello, Mr. Hunter," Joe said, extending his hand.

Mr. Hunter was a small, slender man, with brown hair and shifty blue eyes. He wiped his hands on his trousers before shaking Joe's. "Glad to meetcha. Name's Frank. Has my boy been givin' you trouble?"

"No, not at all. Could we go some place and talk?"

"C'mon in," he said grudgingly and opened the screen door.

"Jimmy, you and Frankie stay out here and play," Joe said.

Inside, the light was so dim that his eyes had to adjust to the darkness. The room was a combination of living, dining, and kitchen areas. On the right side was a door to a bedroom, and a ladder to a loft was on the left.

At first he didn't see the woman standing by the stove, stirring the contents of a black pot. She was small and dressed in a loose-fitting cotton dress. Hanging to her skirt was a filthy little boy who had a thumb in his mouth.

"Cora, this is Frankie's coach at school."

"Glad to meetcha," she said, and continued stirring.

"Same to you," Joe said, smiling.

"What are you wanting to talk to me about?" Mr. Hunter inquired. "Have a chair," he added, pulling one out from the table for Joe and then sitting on another one.

"How long have you lived in our area?" Joe asked.

"We moved here from over in Arkansas last winter."

"Have you started going to church yet?"

"No, we don't have decent clothes to wear to church," he said.

"You can come in what you have," Joe said. "But if you're not comfortable in them, we have a good thrift shop with reasonable prices for clothes and household items."

"We can't even afford cheap prices. Barely have enough to feed these young 'uns."

"Would you be offended if some of our people helped you?"

Mr. Hunter scratched his head. "Don't like to accept charity."

Joe was surprised by this answer. His opinion of the man changed. Maybe there was some good in him.

"You could pay us back when you can, or you could work it out. What kind of work are you in?"

"If I had tools I could do carpentry, painting, fence-mending, most any odd job."

"I'll introduce you to some folks in need of help with odd jobs, and they would gladly help you with food and clothes in exchange," Joe said.

"I'd shore appreciate that," he said. "How is Frankie doing in baseball?"

"He's doing well. Have you been to any of our games?"

"Naw. Haven't had time for such."

"Today Frankie didn't do very well during practice."

"Is that right?"

"He seemed to be in some pain, so after practice I took him into my office and had him raise his shirt."

Mr. Hunter's eyes dropped, and he hung his head. "He deserved a whuppin'," he said.

"With a belt across his back?" Joe asked.

"Maybe I overdid it, but he made me so angry."

"Frank, were you ever beaten with a belt?"

He looked at Joe with anguish in his eyes and said, "Yeah, my paw beat me somethin' fierce when I was a young 'un. Guess that's where I larned it. Makes me feel bad after I've done it to Frankie, though."

"Would you like to break that habit?"

"How?"

"Some men get together with a doctor who can help them overcome this fault. They meet once a month in Wolfeton. Would you like to join them?"

"I dunno. How would I get there?"

"Can you get to the doctor's office in Oak Grove?"

"Yeah, my old car can get me that far."

"If you are there by ten o'clock this Saturday morning, you can ride in a station- wagon with some others from here. All of them have the same problem as you. It's like Alcoholics Anonymous. They meet in a room at the hospital in Wolfeton and talk over their difficulties. The doctor listens and only offers advice when asked."

"I dunno," he said, shaking his head.

"Frank, I offer this solution as a friend, but if you don't follow this plan, and if you keep beating Frankie, I'll have to report you to the police chief and the social workers."

"Okay, okay. I'll be there. Will you help me get some work?" he asked, and this time his blue eyes looked steadily into Joe's gray ones. "I need to work to support my family."

Joe saw a change in Frank as hope filled his heart. All he needed was a chance to work, Joe believed, and it would straighten out his life.

"Sure. I built a tool shed, but haven't had time to paint it. Would you come Thursday? Bring your wife, and my wife can take her to the thrift shop to fit the family with clothes, and also to the grocery store." Joe took out a small notebook and wrote directions to his house, tore the page out, and handed it to him.

"Thanks, I'll be there."

On the way home Jimmy said, "Boy, I'm glad I don't have to live there. I feel sorry for Frankie."

"Jimmy, I want you to take Frankie under your wing and be a friend to him. Would that be hard to do?"

"Well, the boys don't care much for him because he acts kinda funny and doesn't smell very good."

"I'll have a talk with him about personal hygiene, and you invite him to do things with you. Maybe he acts funny because he's shy and doesn't feel welcome among you. All the kids like you, and they'll accept him if you do."

"Okay, Dad."

Joe glanced at his son with pride. It was true. Jimmy won everyone's heart with no effort. He was friendly and easygoing and found no faults in others.

Joe remembered how shy he himself had been when he first came to Oak Grove at the age of eight. His parents and young sister had been killed in a car wreck, and he had come here to live with his aunt and uncle. Uncle Dan, like Mr. Hunter, had beaten him on the slightest excuse, and his Aunt Peg, an alcoholic, had been unable to stop him. In fact, he beat her occasionally also. Everyone knew it, but no one put a stop to it. This had made him determined to stop child and wife abuse whenever he found it. He had started this therapy group on his own, and a Christian psychologist had gotten interested and had asked to help.

When he was a boy, Maggie's parents had wanted him to live with them, but he couldn't leave his aunt to face his uncle alone. Maggie's brother Bob had befriended him, and all the other children had accepted him because of that. He knew that if Jimmy made a friend of Frankie, the others would follow suit.

When they got home, Maggie was cleaning the kitchen. "You're late," she said. "We've eaten, but I have your food warming in the oven. You must have had a good practice. Wash up, Jimmy."

"Okay," Jimmy said, and left the room humming to himself.

Joe looked ashamed. "I should've called you, but I was upset. One of my players, a new boy, was not doing well. I discovered he had welts on his back from a belting by his father."

"How terrible!" Maggie exclaimed.

"We took him home, and I had a talk with the man. He's going to join the support group. By the way, he'll be here Thursday morning to paint the new tool shed, and I'm going to try to get him more jobs around town. He needs work to care for his family, and that should help keep him from becoming frustrated and taking it out on the boy. His wife is coming with him. I hope you don't mind, but I told them that you would take her to the thrift shop and grocery store for his payment. That way we'll be sure the money will go for the right things."

"That's fine with me," Maggie said. "I had other plans, but they can wait. This is more important."

"I'm hoping we can eventually get them in church," he added.

"Maybe his wife could come to our women's Bible study coffee," she said as she took meat loaf out of the oven, put some on each plate, added mashed potatoes and carrots, and placed them on the kitchen table.

"Good idea," Joe said. Looking around he asked, "Where are Corley and Allison?"

"Mrs. Ashley invited them over for dinner. I'm glad that they're getting better acquainted, but I still don't understand why Allison doesn't tell them that she's their granddaughter." She took a bottle of milk and a green salad out of the refrigerator and put them on the table.

"She will eventually, I think. We mustn't rush her. She probably has a good reason that we don't know about."

Jimmy bounced into the kitchen and said, "Something sure smells good! Dad, you better wash up so we can eat."

Chapter X

Wednesday morning after Joe and the children left for school, Meg and Allison cleaned the kitchen and straightened the rest of the house.

"I'm glad you want to go to the Bible coffee with me today, Allison," Meg said. "It'll be at Mary Lou's house."

"Is it okay to bring Corley?" Allison asked anxiously.

"Sure. There will be other small children, and we take turns watching them."

"Will Mrs. Ashley be there?"

"She usually comes if they aren't too busy in the store. Women from all the churches are welcome."

Mary Lou lived in a two-storey brick and stucco Tudor-style house, located in the newest part of town. An attractively landscaped lawn, with trimmed bushes and a variety of bright flowers, added to its charm. The decor inside was early English with delicately tinted, matching colors in the lamps, elegant sofas and chairs, rugs, and walls. Mahogany tables, china cabinets, and other hardwood pieces gave warmth to the room. A large oil painting of the family hung over the brick and wood fireplace. Allison had met Brock Vandenberg at church and thought him handsome and distinguished looking. Besides the parents and two girls in the portrait, a young blond blue-eyed boy of about eight smiled down at her.

"What a lovely family!" Allison exclaimed.

"Thank you," Mary Lou said. "You haven't met our son, Van, have you? He's named after his father, grandfather, and great-grandfather, which makes him Brock, the fourth, but we have always called him Van. Makes it simpler with so many Brocks around."

The women gradually began to arrive until there were ten present, but Mrs. Ashley didn't come. Besides Corley, there were three other small children.

"It's my turn to keep the children," said Donna Lyons, the Baptist pastor's wife. She had her ten-month-old son Joshua with her.

"Bring all the children down to the recreation room in the basement," Mary Lou said and led the way.

"This room should keep them entertained," Allison said as she looked around. It was full of gym equipment, a ping-pong table, pool table, and shelves of games, puzzles, and books. One corner was devoted to children's toys and books, and it was here that the mothers seated their youngsters.

When they returned upstairs, the other women were seated around the dining-room table with their Bibles, notebooks, and pens. Meg had brought an extra Bible for Allison. She gave her paper from her notebook, and Allison took a pen out of her purse. Meg introduced her to the others. Many had already met her, and the rest had heard about her.

Mary Lou brought in a tray laden with coffee, cream, and sugar. The cups and saucers were already on the table. While they drank the coffee they made small talk about the everyday happenings in their lives.

After they finished the coffee and everything was cleared away, one of the ladies opened the meeting with prayer. Then Mary Lou said, "I would like to read the Ninety First Psalm." Turning to Allison she explained, "We always read a psalm first, and the hostess chooses it."

Allison listened to the beautiful words about trusting God and wished she could. How wonderful to feel safe under His wings! Did she have that much faith? She knew that she hadn't been trusting God to keep her safe or help her with her fears. Although she considered herself a Christian, she didn't really know God that well.

Meg led the discussion, which was based on the first chapter of the Book of James. Even though Allison didn't understand much of the scripture, she was too embarrassed to ask questions. There were new versions written in modern English which made the Bible easier to understand. She vowed to buy one and start reading it.

She had been impressed that every morning after breakfast at the Sullivan home, when Joe read a passage of scripture, the whole family discussed it. If any of the children had a problem at school, they were encouraged to apply the lesson to it.

One woman in the group expressed her unhappiness with some of her trials, but she saw how it was increasing her faith. "I have to depend upon the Lord," she said.

During the discussion Meg said, "Sin is not only the wrong things we do, it is also a lack of faith in God's power to provide the help we need."

On the way home after the meeting Meg commented, "You're awfully quiet, Allison. Is something wrong?"

"I think I'll get a new Bible. One that's written in modern English. It will be easier to read and understand."

"You're welcome to use any of ours. We have several versions, but it would be best to get one of your own."

"Thank you. Will you help me choose one?"

"Yes, of course. Tomorrow a family who needs assistance is coming to our house. The man will paint the tool shed Joe built, and I'll take his wife to the thrift shop for clothes and to the grocery store for food. This is the way we'll pay him to make sure the money goes for his family's needs. Would you like to go?"

"Yes. I didn't know you had a thrift shop here. Does it belong to the church?"

"No. It's run by volunteers, and the whole town cooperates. We charge a little, so no one need feel as if they are accepting charity."

"Do you take them to the Ashleys' grocery store?"

"Yes, and the Ashleys give them a ten percent discount on their grocery bill. If Joe feels the man deserves more pay than we spend, he makes up the difference with cash. He intends to ask around if anyone else can use this man."

"Does this happen often?"

"Not too often. Some families can't seem to make a go of it and need assistance occasionally. Joe thinks this man really wants to work."

That night in bed Allison couldn't sleep for thinking about her fears and lack of faith. While Corley was ill, she had been worried about him and didn't think of the murder. But lately she had been obsessed with it. She wished she had enough faith to trust God to keep her safe. It would be so comforting to feel protected under His wings, where nothing could harm her or Corley.

Another thought entered her mind. She should come forward and be a witness for the police. Maybe they couldn't use the car tag evidence without her personal testimony. But there was a spy for the murderers in the police force, and she couldn't take that chance!

She slid out of bed onto her knees and prayed, "Father, help me to trust in you. Please help my unbelief. Amen."

Then she climbed back in bed and went to sleep.

Chapter XI

As the days passed, Allison began relaxing. The scene in the garage dimmed in her mind, and she began to feel safe. She helped Meg with the housecleaning, cooking, laundry, gardening, and officially became the assistant coach on Callie's softball team.

When the children were home they played with Corley and kept him entertained. Callie was like a little mother to him, and he loved the extra attention.

Meg showed Allison pictures of Sylvia and their friends taken from the time they were small through their high-school years.

"Living in this small town, I guess you and my mother knew each other all of your lives, didn't you?"

Meg laughed and said, "Well, not exactly. I saw her around town at different functions, but I really didn't get acquainted with her until we were in kindergarten together. To tell you the truth, I didn't like her very much at first. Sylvia's dresses remained perfectly pressed and clean all day. In the winter, her long white stockings didn't bag around her knees or ankles. I was a tomboy and I thought she was too prissy. For me playing tag or other rough games with the boys was a lot more fun than sitting down bouncing a ball and picking up jacks. By the end of the morning, my dresses were usually rumpled and dirty."

"Sounds as if you had a lot of fun," Allison commented with a smile.

"I thought so at the time. As you know, Sylvia was an only child and her parents went out of their way to make everything perfect for her. On a sunny Saturday in April, they planned a spectacular party for her sixth birthday. There was a clown, balloons, ice- cream, and a beautifully decorated chocolate cake. Everyone in our class was invited. I came dressed in my best clothes. My mother had warned me to stay clean and out of trouble. She remained to help with the party.

"At first, the party was a great success. We laughed and enjoyed the antics of the clown. After he left, we played a few games. Then it happened! I got into a fight with one of the boys. Before anyone could separate us, the boy shoved me and I landed in the middle of the chocolate cake.

"'You did that on purpose!' I yelled at him."

Allison was holding her sides and laughing.

"As you can imagine, my mother was mortified. She apologized to the Ashleys as she jerked me up and hurried me to the car. When we got home, she cut a switch and whipped my bare legs."

"Ouch!" Allison said.

"Yeah, it hurt all right. At school the next Monday, Sylvia told me that the best part of the party was when I fell into the cake. We laughed together and that was the beginning of our friendship."

Meg pointed to another picture. "This is Sue, one of Sylvia's and my best friends. She's Doug Gregory's older sister."

Allison looked at the picture curiously. Sue had a round face, short curly black hair, and large brown eyes. In every picture she had little bows on each side of her head.

Meg said, "She always wore those bows to match her dresses or Sloppy Joe sweaters. That was what the sweaters were called in those days."

Pointing to the picture of a petite blonde girl, she said, "This is Amy, the one married to my brother Bob. Here is a family picture taken before the war. My little brother Johnny is now married and has four children. He's a mechanic and owns a garage in Wolfeton."

"Your mother was beautiful, Meg, and you look like her."

"Yes, she was, and thank you for the backhanded compliment," Meg said with a twinkle in her eye.

When Allison looked through Meg's yearbook, she was proud that her mother had been valedictorian of her class. Although she wasn't as pretty as the other girls, she had more style.

"I don't look like my mother, do I?" she commented.

"No, you look like your father," Meg replied.

*****

A week after Corley's discharge from the hospital, Allison took him to the doctor for a check-up. The doctors' offices were located in an older, white frame house a block from Main Street. Dr. Gregory was friendly with Allison and pleased with Corley's progress. He asked about her husband, and she told him that he had been killed in Vietnam.

"I noticed your ring," he said.

"I haven't taken it off yet," she said. "It makes him seem still alive if I wear it."

The doctor glanced at her in a contemplative manner.

Chapter XII

Thursday morning Allison was humming as she dressed herself and Corley for the trip to the circus. She put on a pair of jeans and a cotton shirt and pulled her hair back into a pony-tail. This is getting to be my uniform, she thought. It wasn't one of Meg's days to teach but she had gone to school to practice the glee club for the spring concert. Allison had told her about meeting Nick in town and about the scheduled event.

"That'll be fun for Corley," she had said. "His first circus! Wish I could go with you. I may talk Joe into taking all of us this Saturday. You and Corley could go again if we go."

The doorbell rang just as Allison put on the finishing touches of her make-up.

"You're ready?" Nick asked when she answered it. "I thought I'd have to wait awhile."

Allison laughed and said, "Everything went smoothly. Corley is excited about the circus. Joe told him all about the elephants, monkeys, lions, and tigers that he would see. He's in a hurry to go so he cooperated with me."

"See elephums!" Corley exclaimed with shining eyes.

They arrived in Wolfeton in time to see the circus parade through the main streets of the town. Allison became nearly as excited as Corley. She had gone to many circuses in Chicago, and it still thrilled her to see the glitter and glamour of the big event.

Nick grinned at her and said, "I think I'm taking two children to the circus."

After the parade, they went to the grounds near the circus tent where food vendors had set up shop in small booths. Wooden tables and benches scattered among them provided places to rest and eat.

"It's hard to decide what to eat," Allison said as she surveyed the choices. The enticing aroma of hamburgers, hotdogs, and corn dogs filled the air. Snow cones, cotton candy, and funnel cakes were also available.

"What's that?" Allison pointed to a sign that read "Indian tacos."

"You haven't eaten until you've tried one of those. It's Indian fry bread covered with hamburger meat and topped with lettuce, tomatoes, onions, cheese, and a special taco sauce. It's good and filling, too."

"I think I'll try it. What do you want, Corley?"

"Want hotdog," Corley said.

While they ate Nick kept her laughing by his witty conversation. Halfway through the meal, however, she had an eerie feeling that she was being watched. She whirled around and met the hostile black eyes of a squat dark man. The other man in the garage! He had found her. Her face blanched with fright.

Nick looked at her and saw naked fear in her eyes. "What's the matter?" he asked.

"That man over there is staring at me as if he hates me."

The man turned and lumbered off.

"Oh, that's just old Willie. He hates everyone, but he's harmless."

"Has he ever been to Chicago?"

"Willie? No, he's a home-grown crosspatch. I doubt he's ever been out of this county. Does he resemble someone you know?"

"No...not exactly."

"Well, put him out of your mind. He won't bother you."

Allison hoped Nick was right. She was relieved that he was a local man, but she still watched Willie out of the corner of her eye.

After they ate, they went on the circus grounds to see the different animals. Corley was most impressed with the elephants.

When the ticket booth opened, Nick bought their tickets and they entered the large tent. The circus was everything that Allison remembered. The antics of the clowns, the trapeze artists, the animal acts, magnificently decorated prancing horses, and the feats of the trained elephants were all as she recalled. Allison and Corley both laughed and clapped their hands at the clowns. Allison gasped and held her breath at times during the performance of the trapeze artists.

Nick seemed to enjoy watching their reactions more than he did the performers.

After the circus ended, Nick took them to a restaurant for dinner. Allison had objected because she thought he had spent enough money on them, but he insisted.

They dawdled over coffee while they talked. Two topics weren't mentioned: Vietnam and the events leading up to Allison's arrival in Oak Grove. Corley was worn out and slept on the bench beside Allison.

"Have you been to the Gaslight Theater here in Wolfeton? "Nick asked.

"No. I didn't know there was one here."

"They have very good meals and amusing plays. Would you like to go with me next Tuesday?"

"Yes, if the Sullivans don't mind tending to Corley."

When they left the restaurant, Nick bore Corley to the car and placed him in his car seat. At the Sullivans' house, Nick carried him in and said, "Where do you want me to lay him?"

"Give him to me and I'll put him to bed," Joe said. Corley never woke up during the exchange of hands or when Joe placed him in his crib.

He came back in the living-room and said, "He's worn out. Bet he had a good time."

Nick drank coffee and joined in small talk with them. Before he left he said, "I'd like to take Allison to the Gaslight Dinner Theater in Wolfeton next Tuesday. I know she'd enjoy it."

"If that's a hint for us to babysit Corley, we'll be glad to," Joe said.

Allison accompanied him to the door and said, "Thanks for a most enjoyable day. That circus was great."

"I'll see you next Tuesday at five o'clock," Nick said.
*****
The next day, Allison took Corley to Dr. Gregory's office for his second visit. The doctor seemed glad to see them and said, "You're looking good, Corley. What've you been up to lately?"

Corley's eyes grew big with excitement and he said, "See elephums!"

"See what?" the doctor asked, puzzled.

"Elephums! Me and Nick and Mama see elephums."

Allison laughed at his baffled expression and said, "Nick Nichols took us to the circus in Wolfeton yesterday. Corley liked the elephants best."

"What did the elephants do, Corley?" he asked.

Corley crouched down and then stood up, bent his knees in a sitting position, and thrust his arms forward.

"Oh, they sat up, did they?" he said and laughed.

"Show him what the lions did," Allison said.

Corley crouched down again, but when he reared up he made claws out of his hands, bared his teeth, and hissed like a cat.

Dr. Gregory laughed again and said, "You give a good imitation, Corley."

He examined Corley thoroughly and then pronounced him cured.

"I won't need to see him in my office again," he said.

Allison was thankful that Corley was well but knew she would miss the visits with Dr. Gregory. From now on she would only see him in the choir on Sundays.

Chapter XIII

A week later on Friday evening the telephone rang and Meg answered it.

"It's for you," she said, handing the phone to Allison.

Fear shot through her. She knew Nick was working this evening. Who knew she was here? Had they caught up with her?

Meg noticed her hesitancy and white face and said, "Allison, what's the matter with you? It's only Doug Gregory."

Hands trembling with relief, she took the phone and said, "Hello."

Dr. Gregory began without preamble, "Do you like band concerts?"

"Yes. I haven't been to one in a long time."

"There's one in the park tomorrow night. Would you like to go with me?"

"May I bring Corley?"

"Sure. I'll be by for you at seven."

"We'll be ready," Allison said and slowly replaced the phone in its cradle, after his abrupt "Good-bye" was followed by the click of his cutting off.

"Dr. Gregory wants me to attend a band concert in the park with him," she said in wonderment.

"I don't blame him," Joe said. "If I weren't married to this beautiful woman, I would want to take you to a concert."

"I'm glad you qualified that statement," Meg said with a laugh. "We can keep Corley for you. He might get restless before the concert ends."

"Our girl is quite popular with the young men around town," Joe joked. "Two dates with Nick and now another beau pops up.

Allison blushed. She had enjoyed the Tuesday night date with Nick at the Gaslight Theater. He was a good friend and amusing to be with, but she didn't take him seriously. She knew he flirted with any woman. However, he had looked at her with admiration and said, "This is the first time I've seen you in anything but jeans and a pony-tail. You're one gorgeous high-class gal!"

The next evening Allison was in a quandary about what to wear. Meg assured her that anything would be appropriate.

"It's casual," she said. "You can wear shorts, long pants, jeans, a skirt, or a dress."

Allison chose a print dress of spring flowers on a white background and white sandals. She wore her shoulder-length black hair down and applied her make-up flawlessly.

"You look so fresh and beautiful," Meg sighed.

Sarah had a date that evening to go to a party with Bill Bradford, a senior and pitcher for the baseball team. She came into the living-room in a new blue dress and twirled around in front of them.

"How do you like my new dress?" she asked.

"It brings out the color in your eyes," Allison remarked.

"Looks good on you," Meg added.

"You look like a princess," Joe said fondly.

The doorbell rang, and Sarah said, "That's Bill. Tell him I'll be ready in a minute."

"You look like you're ready now," Joe commented.

"I don't want to seem eager," she declared and ducked out of the room.

Joe opened the door. "Come in, Bill. She'll be here in a minute."

"Hi, Coach," Bill said. He came into the room and stopped in his tracks when he saw Allison.

"Bill, meet our guest, Allison Ames," Joe said. "Allison, this is our star pitcher, Bill Bradford."

Allison held out her hand and said, "Glad to meet you, Bill."

Bill's eyes were wide open with admiration. "Gl-glad to meetcha," he stuttered as he crossed the room and took her hand. He kept hold of it until she smilingly disengaged it. At that moment, Sarah came into the room.

"Bill, I'm ready," she said.

"Huh?" he said, still gazing at Allison.

"I said I'm ready!" she answered.

When he didn't move, she walked over to him and pinched his arm with her sharp fingernails, and repeated, "I'm ready!"

"Ouch!" he said, rubbing the spot. And then, seeing the look of annoyance on her face, he tucked her arm in the crook of his, said, "Good-bye," and they left.

"I wish she wouldn't do that to my best pitcher," Joe complained.

At seven Doug Gregory rang the doorbell, and Callie ran to let him in. He was casually dressed in brown slacks and an open-collared tan sport shirt.

"Hello, Doug," Meg said. "You look nice."

"Thanks, Meg. Hi, Joe," he said. "Still giving the boys a vigorous workout at school?"

"Doing my best," Joe said. "You're taking out the next to the prettiest gal in town. Have a good time."

"Corley not going?" he asked.

"No. Eat ice-cream," said that little individual, holding on to Joe's pant leg.

"I see he's been bribed," Doug said, laughing.

"Would I do that?" Joe asked innocently.

"Yeah!" They all answered together.

Allison kissed Corley, and then left with Doug. He helped her into his late model green Buick and drove out of the driveway onto the country lane. She leaned back in the soft cushioned seat and glanced at his handsome profile as he kept his eyes intently on the road.

"What kind of music does the band play?" she asked.

"All types," he replied. "Marches, classical, golden oldies, musicals, and even some rock. What do you like?"

"Everything you mentioned."

Although the night was clear, the wind felt a little chilly when they reached the park, and Allison was glad she had thrown her white sweater across her shoulders at the last minute.

As they walked down the path to a bench, people greeted them. Everyone seemed to know her name and that she was staying with the Sullivans. He was greeted as Doug or Dr. Doug.

"How do all these people know me, Dr. Gregory?" she whispered. "I've met only a few of them."

"Call me Doug. You haven't lived in a small town before, have you?"

"No."

"Welcome to the small town rapid news service."

The band members were tuning their instruments as they reached a bench and sat down. Twilight was descending, and the lights around the park came on. Light bulbs outlined the bandstand gazebo, making a pretty picture.

When they began to play, Allison sat quietly enjoying the music and the cool breeze blowing across the park. When the band took a break, Doug bought lemonade from a stand, and they made small talk as they sipped it.

"You're from Chicago?" he asked.

Allison looked startled. "How did you know?"

"I could tell by your Midwestern accent, and I guessed a large town."

"Oh, am I that obvious?" she said with a small laugh and decided there was no use trying to fool anyone, even though she would rather not be connected with Chicago.

On the way home he asked her if she were doing anything Sunday afternoon.

"No, I don't think the Sullivans have plans," she said.

"If you would like, I could pick you and Corley up about two and take you to the park. There's a children's playground with swings, slides, and even a sandbox."

"Thank you. We would both like that."

When they reached the Sullivans' house, he walked her to the door, waited until she had opened it, and then said, "Good night. See you tomorrow," and left.

What a strange man, she thought.

Corley ran to meet her. She picked him up, hugged him, and said, "I'd better get you to bed."

"Did you have a nice time?" Meg asked.

"Yes, I enjoyed the concert immensely. It surprised me, though, when everyone we met knew my name and where I was staying."

"That's the way small towns are," Joe said. "Tomorrow there really will be a buzzing. Everyone will be discussing the doctor's new date."

"Oh, no!" Allison exclaimed. "He invited us to go to the park Sunday afternoon, so Corley can play on the swings and slides. I don't want to cause talk."

"Whatever you do or don't do in this town will cause talk," Meg said. "But it isn't vicious gossip. People are just interested in anything new that happens, and they are extremely concerned about Doug."

"Why Doug?" she asked.

"We all want him to marry a girl who will settle in this town," Meg said. "We don't want to lose a good doctor. Dr. Newberry isn't getting any younger."

That night, after she had gone to bed, Allison lay awake thinking about Doug. He had not put his arms around her or given any indication that he liked her in a special way. She wondered why he had asked her out.

The next morning she went to church again with the Sullivan family. She wore a two-piece rose-colored dress with her pearls and matching pearl drops in her ears. Doug was in the choir, and she caught his eyes on her several times during the service. Once she glanced across the auditorium and met the stare of a pretty, fair-haired woman.

At the park playground, Doug pushed Corley in the swing, caught him coming down the slide, rode on the merry-go-round with him, and worked one end of the teeter-totter while Allison held him on the other.

Finally Allison put Corley in the sandbox with a bucket and shovel to give Doug a rest. They sat on the bench to watch him. Occasionally people passed by and nodded and spoke to them.

"How do you like being a surrogate father?" she asked teasingly.

"I think I'm pretty good at it," he said. "If you don't mind my asking, how long has your husband been gone?"

"Brad left for Vietnam a year and a half ago, and it has been nearly a year since he was killed."

"Corley hasn't had a father that he can remember, then?"

"No, just my father. Brad's parents are both dead. My mother died a few weeks ago."

He looked at her with sympathy and said, "You have had it rough. I'm sorry that I came down on you so hard when Corley was sick. It was mostly that I was afraid I couldn't save him."

"I'm so grateful for all you did for him," she said.

"I give all the credit to the Lord. He's the One who pulled him through," he said humbly.

"That's a strange thing for a doctor to say," Allison said.

"I always pray for guidance in my care of patients," he said. "Couldn't get through a day without His help. I wish He'd help me control my tongue better."

"Maybe you need to help yourself on that," she said.

"You're right," he said ruefully. "Could I take you to dinner and a theater in Wolfeton on Thursday evening? *Harvey* is playing. I'm going to be on call next weekend and will stay at the hospital."

"Yes, I always enjoy that play."

Two young women strolled by and stopped in front of them. Allison recognized one of them as a nurse at the Wolfeton hospital.

"Hello, Dr. Gregory," the nurse said tossing back her thick, curly auburn hair. "And Mrs. Ames, how nice to see you. How's Corley?" Then she saw him in the sandbox, and said, "Hi, Corley. You look lots better than when I saw you last."

"Hi!" he said, smiling at her.

"Hello, Nurse Walters," Allison said.

"Call me Kim," she said. "This is my friend Beth Adams. She teaches second grade here at the Oak Grove school."

Beth was a pretty woman with brown hair and blue eyes. "Glad to meet you," she said.

Doug had stood up when they came, and now he asked them if they wanted to sit down.

"No," Kim replied. "It's such a pretty day that we came here to walk and enjoy it."

Allison had the feeling that Doug had probably dated them in the past, and the young woman in church, also. After all, he was young, handsome, and eligible.

Later, during the evening services at church, Doug sat by Allison. She was beginning to enjoy his closeness.

Chapter XIV

On Monday, the Ashleys invited Allison and Corley for dinner. Knowing their kinship to her, Allison was always glad to visit with them. After dinner, she asked if she could see the scrapbook of newspaper clippings about Sylvia. Mrs. Ashley was happy to show them to her, and she took her into the den where they were kept. While they looked at them, Mr. Ashley entertained Corley in the living-room with the toys and books they had bought for him.

Impressed by the newspaper accounts of Sylvia's cases Allison said, "Sylvia was a brilliant lawyer, wasn't she?"

"Yes, and we were very proud of her," Mrs. Ashley said. "We weren't happy when she went to Chicago. At first she worked in a law firm and studied law in the evenings. We hoped she would get tired of it and come home, get married, and raise a family. When that didn't happen, we gave in and sent her to college and law school, full-time. I now realize it was for the best. She met Bernard Bachman, who had lost his wife to cancer, and fell in love. They married but were not able to have children. He had two by his previous marriage so didn't care. Would you like to see Sylvia's photo album?"

"Yes, I would," she replied. "I saw some of Meg's pictures and her high school yearbook. Sylvia received many honors, didn't she?"

"Yes, she did," Mrs. Ashley said proudly. "I have her photo album of pictures after they graduated. Sylvia gave it to me when she came home the last time."

Sitting side by side on the sofa, Mrs. Ashley turned the pages and described the events in the photographs.

"These are pictures of the girls leaving on the bus for Oklahoma City. This one is Sylvia and you know Meg. The other one is Sue Gregory, Dr. Gregory's older sister."

There were pictures of the three in Oklahoma City with different servicemen. The one that caught Allison's eye was Sylvia and a tall, handsome airman with black hair and dark eyes. Trying not to be obvious, Allison asked her if she knew any of the servicemen's names.

"No, Sylvia said it was a long time ago, and she couldn't remember their names."

The last pictures were taken after the war when Sylvia was home on visits from Chicago. In several of the pictures, Brock Vandenberg had his arm around Meg. Allison commented on this.

"We thought they would marry when he graduated from college, but when Joe came home three years after the war was over, it became obvious that he was the one she loved," replied Mrs. Ashley. "Sylvia said that she had suspected it all along, because Meg kept putting Brock off. Even told him to find someone else."

The clock struck eight, and Allison told her that she had better get Corley home to bed. They went into the living-room and found Mr. Ashley asleep in his lounge chair with Corley sleeping on his lap and a picture-book about to slide off on the floor.

Later, when Corley was in his crib at the Sullivan's house, Allison asked Meg if she reminded her of Sylvia.

"Yes, you remind me of her, the way you walk and the way you cock your head when you're listening to someone. Just little things, but mainly your sense of style."

"We were looking at the scrapbook of clippings, and Mrs. Ashley remarked that I reminded her of Sylvia. Isn't that uncanny? I don't look anything like her. She also showed me Sylvia's photo album of you girls in Oklahoma City. One picture was of Sylvia with a tall, handsome black-haired airman. Was that my father?"

"I never saw the picture, but it probably was."

"I also saw pictures of you and Brock Vandenberg looking very chummy," she said, grinning mischievously.

"Yes, we dated," Meg said with a smile. "I told him from the start that we were good friends, but I didn't love him enough to marry him. Joe was always the one I loved. When I was a kid, I would follow Joe and my brother Bob everywhere, even into the woods, and I found all of their hiding places. Bob would get angry and call me 'Tag-a-long Maggie,' but Joe didn't mind. He always stood up for me."

"Does Mary Lou know about you and Brock?"

"Oh, yes. She told me that Brock told her about me before he brought her here the first time. He was afraid that she would hear it second-hand," Meg said with a laugh. "She thanked me for turning him down and giving her a chance. They are perfect for each other."

On Tuesday, Meg stayed late after school to attend a teachers' meeting. When she arrived home she found Allison in the kitchen starting dinner.

"The mail's on the table," Allison said. "Go ahead and read it. I don't need any help."

Among the usual advertisements and requests for money, Meg found a letter from her friend Sue. Earlier, she had written to Sue about Sylvia's daughter Allison coming to Oak Grove, and the fact that she hadn't yet told the Ashleys she was their granddaughter.

She had also mentioned Corley's illness and that he had been under Doug's care.

In the last paragraph Meg had added, *"Allison seems to be afraid of something, but so far she hasn't confided in us."*

Allison was peeling potatoes when Meg came into the kitchen.

"Uh-oh, you've been found out, Allison," she said. "Doug's mother has written to her daughter, my friend Sue, and told her that he's interested in you. She asked Sue if she knew your mother in Oklahoma City, and she wants to know all about her."

"I wonder what she'll tell her," Allison said.

"That's what Sue is wondering," Meg replied with a laugh.

Chapter XV

Thursday night Allison and Doug went to dinner and then to a comedy at the Wolfeton Playhouse Theater. The actors were good in their parts, and Doug and Allison both laughed until their sides hurt. Allison was surprised to see Doug so relaxed and happy since before that night he always seemed so solemn. He was not at all like the Dr. Gregory that she had first met and disliked.

Again he walked her to the door, waited until she opened it, told her "Good night," and abruptly left.

Corley was in bed asleep, as were the other children, but Meg sat in the living-room with a smile on her face.

"Mike and Luke are coming home this weekend," she said happily. "I've invited Dad and Alice over for a cookout on Saturday."

"Sounds like fun," Allison replied.

The next day when Sarah came home from school she asked, "May I invite Kathy to the cookout?"

"Sure," Meg said.

"She's my best friend," Sarah told Allison.

After she left to make her call, Meg added, "And she has a crush on Mike."

As Meg and Allison cooked supper that evening, they heard loud honking in the front drive. "They're here," Meg laughed and flew through the house to open the door.

Two young men emerged from a late model yellow Mustang. Both had long hair falling around their shoulders. Allison guessed the darker one was Mike. His hair was black, his eyes were as deep a blue as Meg's, and his skin was a lighter tan than his father's. The other youth was fair and had light brown hair and brown eyes. He unlocked the trunk, pulled out a bulging laundry bag, and handed it to Mike, who in turn handed it to Sammy.

"You always bring me a present, don't you, Mike?" Meg laughed, as her oldest son put his arms around her and hugged her.

The other children swarmed around them laughing and talking. Max was barking and jumping on both of the young men. Callie was carrying Corley, and he was holding out his arms to Mike.

"I think you remind him of Dad," Callie said.

"Allison, come and meet Mike and Luke," Meg said.

She had been standing in the doorway while the others welcomed the young men, and now she stepped forward.

"Wow!" Mike exclaimed.

"Yeah!" Luke agreed.

"That doesn't sound very polite," Meg admonished them. "This is Allison Ames, and her son, Corley. Allison, Mike and Luke. You can probably guess which one is Mike."

Mike took her hand and said, "Glad to meet you."

"I am, too," Luke said, taking her other hand.

"Goodbye, Uncle Luke," Mike said jokingly. He liked to tease Luke occasionally by calling him uncle. "Thanks for bringing me home."

"See you tomorrow," Luke said, and reluctantly got in his car and left.

A half hour later, Joe and Jimmy came home from ball practice, and there was more talking and excitement. All through the meal each tried to outtalk the other. Allison had a chance to quietly observe the family. Mike's features were like Joe's, and Sarah resembled Meg with her dark blue eyes, brown curly hair, and fair skin. Sammy had his father's black hair, greenish-gray eyes, and dark skin, while Jimmy was fair with gray eyes. Callie's face had an oriental cast with slanted gray eyes and high cheek-bones. Her complexion was fair and her dark brown hair hung to her shoulders. The main thing Allison noticed was that they cared about each other.

"Why can't I let my hair grow like Mike's?" Jimmy asked. "Most of the boys at school have long hair."

"No one on my baseball team is allowed to have long hair, and that goes for you, too."

"Can I let mine grow?" Sammy asked. "I'm not on the team."

"No, you can't!"

"Why not?"

"Because I said so and I'm the biggest," Joe replied.

After supper, Joe and the boys went out to shoot baskets in the hoop attached to a pole beside the driveway. Mike wore a band around his head to keep the hair out of his eyes, and it emphasized his Indian features. The girls joined them after they cleaned the kitchen and started the dishwasher.

Meg, Allison, and Corley sat on the porch and watched them.

When it got too dark, they all came into the house for lemonade and cookies. At eight, Allison put Corley to bed, and the rest of the children watched television until ten. Then they also went to bed.

Mike stayed in the living-room to talk to his parents. He sat on the couch beside Allison.

"Dad," he said, "what would you think if I came home with an earring in my ear?"

"I think I'd lock the door and keep you out."

"I was afraid that's what you would say," he said gloomily.

"Long hair is bad enough, but I won't put up with any more foolishness," Joe said.

On Saturday morning, Mike went to town to look up friends. Allison helped Meg and the girls clean house, while Sammy and Jimmy mowed and trimmed the lawn. Joe went to town to buy steaks for the cookout.

After lunch, Luke came over. "I thought I'd see if you needed help to get ready for the cookout," he said, eyeing Allison.

"No, we're doing okay," Mike told him.

They spent the next hour vying for Allison's attention, until Meg sent them outside to get the lawn chairs out of the garage and set them up on the deck. Although there was a long wooden table with benches already on it, she had them bring out a folding table also. At four o'clock, Brock Vandenberg brought his daughter Kathy. Her eyes quickly found Mike, but he barely noticed her. He was still caught up in admiring Allison and verbally trying to beat Luke to gain her interest.

"I'd like a word with you, Joe," Brock said, after greeting the rest of them.

The two men withdrew to the opposite end of the deck. Allison couldn't help comparing them. Since it was Saturday, Brock was in casual slacks and a sport shirt. He had a trim, compact build, brown hair, hazel eyes, and classically handsome features. His mien was serious and businesslike. On the other hand, Joe, in jeans and plaid sport shirt, appeared relaxed and at ease as he leaned on the rail of the deck with his arms crossed and listened.

When their business was finished, Brock bade them goodbye and instructed Kathy to call him when she was ready to come home.

"There's no need for that. We'll see that she gets home," Joe said.

At five p.m., Sam and Alice arrived.

"We decided if we wanted to see our son, we had better get up here," Sam said with a smile.

"We brought potato salad and baked beans," Alice added.

"Anything else we can get for you, or do?" Sam asked.

"No, I think everything is under control," Meg replied. "Joe just now put on the steaks, and the table is ready."

"Hey, guys," Sammy said, "let's shoot a few baskets while we're waiting."

"We want to shoot some, too," Sarah said. "If Mom doesn't need us, that is."

"Go ahead and play," Meg said. "We're caught up."

"Do you want to play, Allison?" Mike asked.

"Sure," she said. "I haven't played since high school."

"Come on," Mike said taking her arm. Luke quickly got on her other side as they walked around the house to the goal. Allison saw the disappointed look on Kathy's face but didn't know what she could do about the situation.

Mike and Luke started out trying to be easy on the girls but soon saw Allison was a match for them, so they played rougher. It was good exercise and Allison enjoyed it.

When they were called to come and eat, they came laughing and talking about the game as they washed up at the outside water faucet.

"You need Allison on your team this winter, Dad," Mike said. "She's good!"

"I thought Kathy played well, too," Sarah said.

"Yeah, yeah. You all did good," Mike said as he started filling his plate.

"Aren't you forgetting something, Mike?" Joe asked.

"Sorry," Mike said, and bowed his head, while Joe asked the blessing.

Allison took Corley in the house to wash him because he had been playing with Max. He and the dog were great friends. The others were eating when they returned. She filled her plate and, ignoring the seat between Mike and Luke that had been saved for her, led Corley to a chair near Kathy and Sarah.

"How is your softball practice going?" she asked. "I don't see much of it since I'm coaching on the other team."

"Okay," Kathy said.

"I think we'll have a great team," Sarah said. "Kathy is our best player."

"I saw pictures of your father in Mrs. Sullivan's photo album," Allison said.

"Yes, they were good friends, and still are. He graduated a year ahead of her."

"Your mother didn't graduate from Oak Grove, did she?"

"No. Dad met her in college. She's from Oklahoma City."

"You look like your mother."

"Everyone says I do. Corley is a cute little boy," she said, as he slid down from his chair and walked over to Joe, holding up his hands. Joe picked him up, set him on his lap, and let him eat grapes from his plate.

"He likes men best," Allison said.

"Sarah told me about his father. I was sorry to hear it."

"Thank you."

When they finished eating, the women cleared the table and put the food away. Since they used paper plates and plastic dinnerware, except for steak knives, there weren't many dishes to wash. The men were talking sports when they got back.

By eight p.m. Corley's eyes were drooping, so Allison put him to bed. When she returned, Joe was explaining the business proposition that Brock had discussed with him.

"Some of the businessmen in town want to put in a golf-course. They've found available property and are trying to raise funds. May try to pass bonds. Have they approached you, Sam?"

"Yes, but I'm not sure I want to go in on it," Sam replied. "What did you tell him?"

"That I would talk it over with Maggie, and we'd pray about it. If we had one here, folks would come from Wolfeton to play, and we could still use theirs and have a choice of two. That one is getting crowded."

Sammy was listening avidly, and said, "I want one here, and I could learn to play. Maybe someday I could be a pro."

"You help by praying about it then, and we'll see what God wants us to do with our money."

"I need to call my dad to come after me," Kathy said when the clock struck nine.

"No, Mike can take you home," Joe said. "Here are my car keys, Mike." He tossed them to him.

Good, Allison thought. *Maybe that will make up for her disappointment with the lack of attention he has paid her.*

However, the next day in church, Luke and Mike sat on either side of her, and Kathy and Sarah sat with their other friends. She missed Doug in the choir.

About two in the afternoon, Luke drove up in his Mustang to collect Mike. He entered the house for a few minutes to talk with Allison. Mike came out of his room with his bag full of clean, pressed clothes.

"I'm ready, Luke. Goodbye, you all. See you again soon, Allison."

The family accompanied the boys outside to the car. Luke opened the trunk for Mike to put his bag in. They got in the car and with a wave of their hands, took off in a clatter of gravel.

"You sure dazzled the boys, Allison," Joe said. "Maybe we'll see more of them now."

Later in her bed, Allison thought over the past few days. It had been easy to forget about the danger she was in when she kept busy and others were around. But in the darkness of the night she could see that long lean face with the cold blue eyes.

Would he be coming for her?

Chapter XVI

Monday evening Nick called Allison to invite her and Corley to a Tuesday afternoon horse show.

"The races and other performances are held outdoors on a farm near Wolfeton. I know Corley will enjoy the horses," he said.

"That sounds great!" Allison said.

"Wear your jeans and pony-tail," he said. "I'm not used to dating such a glamorous gal. You intimidate me when you're all dressed up."

"I sure don't want to do that," she said with a laugh.

"Don't eat lunch. They're serving barbecued brisket and ribs with all the trimmings before the events."

The next day Allison caught Nick's gay mood as they headed out into the country and said, "You're mighty happy about this trip, aren't you?"

"Yeah, I haven't been able to get out there lately to ride my horse. I keep him at this farm. They feed him and care for him and I let them rent him out for people to ride. He runs loose in the pasture, too. Gets plenty of exercise."

"I learn something new about you every day. Were you raised on a farm?"

"Yeah, but I'm no farmer. When my parents died, my sister Nicole," he cocked his head at her and grinned, "and I sold the farm. Neither one of us liked farming. I still like horses, though."

Allison burst out laughing. "Your sister's name is Nicole?"

"Yes, we're both Nicks," he said and laughed with her.

They pulled into the parking area and walked to the corral where several people had gathered. "Well, there's Red. Hi, Red," they called to Nick while looking curiously at Allison.

"Who you got with you?" someone asked.

"This is Allison and Corley Ames. I'm not going to try to tell her all of your names. She wouldn't remember them. Too many of you."

Allison received the usual stares of admiration as she smiled at them and said, "Glad to meet you."

At the corral, Nick whistled and one of the horses broke away from the others and neighed as he came up to the fence. Nick had brought sugar cubes with him and offered one to his horse. The horse gently took it from his hand. Corley was excited, and Nick picked him up and let him pet the horse on the nose.

"Say hi to Nicker, Corley," he said.

"Hi, Nicker," Corley said. He turned to Nick and asked, "Ride Nicker?"

"We'll ride him after the races," Nick replied.

"You named your horse Nicker?" Allison asked and laughed. "I thought you had had it with the Nicks!"

"I wanted him to feel part of the family," Nick said and grinned.

When she tasted the barbecued rib, Allison said, "We don't get barbecue this good in Chicago."

"Yeah, this is good old Oklahoma barbecue!"

While they ate the delicious meal she said, "Red? I see you managed to get a nickname after all."

"With this red hair, I was doomed from the start."

Corley enjoyed the whole afternoon of races and the tricks that some of the horses had been taught. His favorites were the barrel races. In this event, barrels were placed in a line and young girls rode their horses in and out between barrels. Sometimes one would accidentally knock over a barrel which made Corley laugh.

When the show was over, Nick saddled his horse and mounted him. Allison handed Corley to him, and they rode around the arena several times.

"Wanna ride?" Nick asked Allison when they returned to her.

"Love to!" He let her step in his hand and boosted her into the saddle. She rode around several times and thoroughly enjoyed the exercise.

*****

Friday night, Doug called and asked Allison if she and Corley would like to take a drive on Saturday. After discussing it, she agreed to go and started planning what she and Corley would wear---blue cotton shorts and shirt for him, and a green slack suit for herself.

"We're going to take the skyline highway from Talihina to Wilhelmina Park in Arkansas and eat lunch at the lodge in the park," she told Meg and Joe.

"It's a beautiful drive," Meg said, "and the food at the lodge is excellent."

"That reminds me, Maggie," Joe said. "Mel Bradford, Brock, Jerry Adams, and I are playing golf on the Wolfeton Golf-Course tomorrow."

"If we build a course here," Meg said, "I may take lessons and play. It would be good exercise."

"You can take lessons now at Wolfeton if you want to," he replied.

"I know, but it would be more convenient if we had one here. Mary Lou wants one here also. I think several women would like to learn to play if we had one."

"Have you been praying for one?" Joe asked teasingly.

Chapter XVII

Saturday was a perfect day for golf. The temperature was in the upper seventies, and there was only a slight breeze. Brock had a pull cart, but the others carried their bags.

Every so often Brock mentioned the course he planned for Oak Grove. He pointed out the rough spots on this course and told how they could be improved.

"You've gotten to be an expert on golf-courses," Joe commented.

"Yes, I've been studying about them lately," Brock replied.

"Has he been hitting you about financing a golf-course at Oak Grove?" Joe asked Mel.

"Yeah, he has," Mel said. "I think it's a good idea."

When they finished the eighteenth hole, they went into the clubhouse for coffee. Brock brought up building a golf-course at Oak Grove again. They discussed the pros and cons for a while. Finally Joe said he would help with it.

"Maggie said she would take lessons if we had one," he said. "I'd like for her to learn the game, then we could play together. It's good exercise. 'Course I'd have to get her one of those sissy little pull carts like Brock's."

"If I don't have to carry my bag, my game is better," Brock defended himself.

"Mel," Joe said, "do you need another man at the lumberyard?"

"Why, are you tired of coaching?" Mel asked with a grin.

"There's this fellow, Frank Hunter, who has a son on my team, and he needs a full-time job to support his family."

"I've heard of him. They say he's a good worker. Where did he come from, and what do you know about him?"

Jerry Adams, a deputy under Chief Bundy, spoke up. "The chief looked up his record when he noticed him around town. You know how he is. Wants to know about all newcomers. It seems he had a little trouble over in Arkansas."

"What kind of trouble?" Joe asked.

"He was accused of robbing a convenience store in a town near where he lived. Since he fit the general description of the thief, he was placed in a line-up, and the clerk picked him. Later the real thief was caught robbing another store, and the clerk admitted he made a mistake. Meanwhile, Hunter had lost his job in a cotton mill, and friends had turned against him. Even though they apologized, he up and moved over here. Took out his savings and bought that little place in the hills."

"A man who has been treated like that deserves a break," Mel said. "I think I can use him."

*****

On the same beautiful day, Allison was in a happy mood and enjoying the spring outing with Doug and Corley. Winding through wooded areas, the highway had occasional cleared spaces to park for a sweeping panoramic view of hills and valleys. Doug stopped at every one of them. Sometimes she could see the curved road miles away, behind them or ahead of them. At one of the stops they saw horses grazing in a field.

Corley pointed at them and shouted, "Horses!" He turned to Doug and said, "Me ride a horse."

"You did?" Doug said. "Where did that happen?"

"Nick and Mama and me saw horses."

Doug looked inquiringly at Allison and she said, 'Nick Nichols took us to see a horse show out on a farm. He has a horse stabled there and we rode it."

"Oh, I see. You're seeing a lot of Nick, aren't you?"

"Not a lot. Once in awhile."

"Horse named Nicker," Corley said. "We ride again next time."

"Corley's talking more, isn't he?" Doug commented.

Lunch at the lodge was every bit as good as Meg had said it would be. Before they ate, they held hands and Doug thanked the Lord for the safe trip and for the food they were about to eat. Corley added, "T'ank you, Jesus." Allison had become used to Joe saying grace at the Sullivan house, and Doug had even asked the Lord's blessing at dinner Thursday evening. It impressed her to see men like Joe and Doug pray.

While they ate, Doug told her a little of the history of the lodge. "It was built in 1897 by the Kansas City, Pittsburgh & Gulf Railroad as a resort for passengers. It's three storeys high and is known as the 'Castle in the Sky.'"

"Why did they name the park Queen Wilhelmina Park?" Allison asked.

"The railroad was backed by Dutch interests, so they named it after the young Dutch queen. They even had a royal suite for her in the vain hope she would visit the area. Three years later the lodge closed and fell into ruin."

"Looks good now."

"Yes, after the area was acquired for a state park in 1957, they reconstructed the lodge, and completed it in 1963."

Corley went to sleep as soon as they started for home. Doug stopped at the vista sights on the side of the highway as they went toward Talihina.

I want you to see it all," he said. "It's been a while since I've been here, so I'm enjoying the sites, too."

At one stop he picked up her left hand and said, "I see you're still wearing your wedding band."

"Yes," she said.

"Why did you come to Oak Grove?" he asked abruptly.

"Wh...what do you mean?" she asked.

"Of all the places in the world, why would a girl from Chicago pick Oak Grove, Oklahoma to visit?"

"I told you. Meg and my mother were good friends."

"I wonder why your mother never came to see Meg," he said.

*****

That night after Allison put Corley in his crib, she thought about going home. It was nearly two months since she had left Chicago. She felt guilty about staying such a long time with the Sullivans. When she mentioned it, they always assured her that they enjoyed her company and wouldn't hear of her going to a motel. Allison tried to pay them, but they wouldn't let her. She insisted on paying for part of the groceries. The cash she had brought with her had run low, and she had gone to the bank and cashed a check. The vice-president, Brock Vandenberg, had approved it. Afterwards she worried that the Chicago police might find her through her cashed check. That's foolish, she told herself, they didn't know her name or the name of her bank.

After Brad had been killed, her father had set up a trust fund for her. Money from it came regularly to her checking account. He didn't want her to get a job and leave Corley in a child care facility. "A baby needs his mother," he had said.

In another few weeks, her father would be home from his trip and would wonder where she was. She had left in such a hurry that she hoped she had left everything in order. Had she stopped the mail? Yes, she remembered dropping a note in her mailbox. Maybe it was time to go back to Chicago. No one could possibly know that she had made that call. By now the killers were probably safely behind bars.

Still, every time she thought about going home, she would see the killer's face and get a cold feeling in the pit of her stomach.

Chapter XVIII

Detective Chuck Brogan left the police station at ten p.m., after twelve hours on duty. Ever since that undercover cop had gotten himself killed, the whole Chicago force had been in an uproar. He stood outside the station and lit a cigarette before going to the parking-lot for his car.

Twenty years he had been on the force, and now he was relegated to a desk job. Men he had trained with and men he had trained were promoted while he was passed over. A big, brawny blond man with a quick temper, he had been demoted for being too rough on those whiny little crooks and dope peddlers. It wasn't right! He was a better detective than most of them on the force.

When he drove out of the parking-lot, he headed for Al's Place. A cold beer and conversation were what he needed. This was not one of the hang-outs of his fellow police officers. He saw enough of them during his work hours, and he didn't like to talk shop, anyway. Sports was his main interest.

Al was behind the bar, and he automatically filled a frosted mug with beer from the barrel at his side and set it on the bar in front of Chuck. The foam on top ran over and coursed down the glass sides of the mug, leaving a wet ring when Chuck picked it up. He took a long draw on it and wiped his lips with the back of his hand.

"Boy! That's good!" he said and belched loudly. "Just wanted to show my appreciation," he joked and headed for a table where several of his cronies sat.

"Hi, boys," he said. "How did the White Sox do today?"

"Got beat by them Yankees!" Bull Muldrow said in disgust.

A lively discussion followed on the merits of the two Chicago teams, and guesses were made about which teams would end up in the Series when fall came.

"Hey, Chuck," a small dark man, nicknamed Shorty, called out to him, "have they found out who killed that cop?"

"You know I can't divulge any police business," Chuck said. "No use askin'. Send another beer over here, Al," he ordered.

At two a.m. Al closed the bar, and all the patrons filed out into the night.

"My old lady will probably have a fit because I stayed out late," Bull said as he headed down the street to his car parked under a street light.

"Mine will be asleep and wait until morning to grouse at me," Shorty said.

"Lucky me," Chuck snickered. "Won't be anyone at home waitin' up for me."

Unobserved by Chuck, a man who had sat at a corner table nursing a beer all evening, got up and left with them. He slipped into a dark Chevrolet and waited until Chuck's car was a block away. Then he followed him.

Chuck drove into the garage of his apartment building and parked in his space. "No one waitin' up for me," he mumbled as he climbed out of his car. His ex-wife, Marge, had gotten enough of his moroseness and occasional abuse and left. "Good riddance!" was his opinion.

The man in the Chevrolet pulled up to an old Ford parked across the street from the building.

"He kept his mouth shut in the bar," he said to the man slouched in it. "Want to go to the alley or stay here?"

"I'm tired of this view. You can stay here, and I'll take the back," he said. Then he quietly drove around the corner with lights out, turned down the alley and parked behind the apartment building.

Chuck fumbled with his keys and finally found the right one to open the door of the building, and then staggered up the stairs. At his apartment door on the second floor, he again had a problem. When he finally got it unlocked and opened, he stumbled in. His hand groped for the elusive light switch, and he let out a string of curses until his fingers finally touched it and illuminated the room.

"Hello, Chuck."

Chuck spun around at the voice and saw a man sitting in his lounge chair, relaxed, with his long legs stretched in front and crossed at the ankles. He held a gin and tonic loosely in his left hand.

"What are you doing here? How did you get in?" he shouted.

"Take it easy," he said. "I just have some unfinished business to take care of."

"I've told you all I know and I gave you a copy of the girl's picture. There's no way I can get the information from those lawyers. You shouldn't have come here."

"Don't worry about the lawyers. I went to their office tonight and found what I needed. Now there is only one more thing I must do."

Chuck looked into his cold blue eyes, and a chill went down his spine.

"What?" he asked belligerently to cover his nervousness.

"Get rid of the only other one who can identify me," he said calmly as a gun with a silencer appeared suddenly in his right hand.

"Why would I finger you?" Chuck asked. "I'd be getting myself in trouble as an accomplice."

"I don't trust you. Any cop who would rat on another one can't be counted on to keep his mouth shut when he's in a pinch. Anyway, you're already in trouble. For the last couple of months you've been followed. Look out the window."

Chuck stepped over to the window and saw the dark Chevrolet parked across the street.

"That's just a neighbor's car," he bluffed.

"You and I both know better. By now there's another car parked in the alley."

"Let's think this through," Chuck said. "You just disappear, and they won't be able to get proof on either one of us."

"I think we should both disappear," he said, and aimed the gun.

"Wait!" Chuck said desperately. "What about Dom Giovanni?"

"He won't talk, because he knows I can reach him anywhere and any time that I find it necessary. Admit it. You're out of your league," he said and fired.

Chuck sprawled on the floor with a bullet hole in the middle of his forehead.

"I think I'll take a nap until it's time to go. May I borrow your bed?" he asked the corpse, and calmly stepping over it, went in the bedroom and lay down on top of the unmade bed.

*****

At five a.m. two more plain-clothes men drove up to relieve the men on surveillance.

"It's been quiet. No one has gone in or out since Chuck went in at two-thirty," they told them.

The men took up their positions, and by seven, people started leaving the building to go to work. At eight, the detective sitting in the car in front, noticed a tall, rangy man in a business suit, with a briefcase in his left hand, come out and walk down the street to catch the bus on the corner.

"He looks familiar," he thought, and then it dawned on him. That was Ned Sutton, a hit man! He got on his radio and put in a call to stop bus 201 and then gave chase. The bus had gone around a corner, and when he and a uniformed cop in a police car caught up with it, Ned had already exited and disappeared.

While several police cars were patrolling the area looking for the hit man, the detective rushed back to the apartment building and rang the bell until it was opened by the gray-headed apartment manager. "Quick! Apartment 2G!" he said.

When there was no answer to his knock, he had the manager open the door with his pass key. Chuck Brogan's body was sprawled on the floor with a bullet hole in the head.

Ned Sutton drove out of the parking garage and passed the stopped bus. He had gotten off around the first corner and entered the garage where he had left his car. The attendant was too busy straining to see what was going on outside to get a good look at him. Now to find Oak Grove, Oklahoma, and Allison Corley Ames at the home of Sylvia Ashley, he thought.

Chapter XIX

Sunday morning Doug was not in the choir. Again Allison was disappointed, but she asked herself sternly if he was the only reason she came to church. She would listen to the young preacher today and not let her mind wander. He read from the Gospel of John about a ruler named Nicodemus who came to see Jesus by night and asked about salvation. It puzzled her when Jesus said that except he be born again, he could not see the Kingdom of God. What did He mean "born again?" Even though Brother Mark read the rest of the text, she didn't understand.

Another verse he read, John 3:16, she had memorized as a child. Mentally, she repeated it with him: "For God so loved the world, that he gave his only begotten Son, that whosoever believeth in him should not perish, but have everlasting life." She did believe that verse, but did not know if she had been born again. Meg could explain it to her.

Allison noticed the Hunter family in church that day. Frankie sat with Jimmy and the other boys his age, while Becky and Betsy sat quietly between their parents. Joe and Meg had been hoping and praying that they would start to church, and she saw the happiness on Meg's face.

When the services were over, people flocked around them in greeting. Allison shook hands with them, and asked Cora if Bryan was in the nursery. Cora nodded her head, and Allison said, "My son, Corley, is there also. We can go together to get them."

In the nursery, the boys had used blocks to make a road and were pushing small cars up and down it. Two little girls were playing with dolls in the housekeeping area.

"Bryan has been very good," Mrs. Brown said. "At first he cried and missed you, but Corley and the other children helped me get him interested in playing with the blocks. During our art time, he drew this picture with crayons." She handed Cora a paper with colorful markings. "Here is a leaflet with our Bible story in it. He liked the story time. You can read this to him at home also." She turned to the children and said, "All of you pick up the toys and put them on the shelves where you found them and then you may go home with your mothers."

It surprised the mothers when the children obediently did as she asked. One of the mothers said, "I wish Nancy would do that at home."

"Just be firm with them and praise them when they cooperate," the teacher said.

*****

At the dinner table, the Sullivans were discussing how glad they were to see the Hunter family in church.

"I noticed that Frankie sat with you and your friends, Jimmy," Joe remarked. "I was glad to see that."

"I was outside when his family drove up, so I invited him to sit with us. Next Sunday he's going to come to Sunday School, if he can get his parents to bring him."

"Is he getting along okay in school?" Joe asked.

"Yes. He doesn't smell bad anymore. Guess you helped him there. His mother is washing their clothes in the laundromat in town now that his father is getting more work. At home they have to get their water out of a deep, open well. It was hard to pull the bucket up and down, so they weren't using any more than they had to."

"I'm pleased that his father is getting a lot of work," Joe said, "and I hope Mel Bradford can use him full-time."

After Corley's nap, Allison received a phone call from Doug.

"I had a medical emergency this morning and missed seeing you in church. Would you and Corley like to go to the park again today?"

"We sure would," she replied.

When Corley tired of playing on the swings and other playground equipment, Allison settled him in the sandbox with his bucket and shovel, and Doug sat beside her on the bench.

Other children, accompanied by their parents, were playing in the park. A curly-headed little girl climbed into the sandbox with her bucket and shovel. She and Corley dug side by side in quiet companionship, and her mother sat on a nearby bench, while Doug and Allison talked.

"No, no!" the woman suddenly shouted. Glancing up, Allison saw Corley standing with his bucket positioned to pour sand over the head of the little girl.

With a cry, Allison jumped up at the same time as the other mother did, and each snatched her child before disaster struck.

Allison apologized to the woman, but she quickly walked away, carrying the little girl who was looking over her shoulder waving and saying "Bye-bye" to Corley.

"That was a naughty thing you almost did, Corley," Allison told him. "You must not pour sand on other children."

She put him back in the sand box , and he unconcernedly emptied his bucket and began filling it again.

"I guess you told him," Doug said with a smile.

"Looks as if I made a big impression," Allison agreed.

"I was sorry that I had to miss church this morning," Doug said. "What was Brother Mark's sermon about?"

"I'm glad you asked," she replied. "I meant to ask Meg, but maybe you can tell me. What does 'born again' mean?"

"Born again means born from above. It's a spiritual birth, and it's the work of God and not the work of man. When we accept Jesus as our Savior, the Holy Spirit gives us this new birth. It's the only way to enter the Kingdom of God."

"I still don't understand," she said. "What do you mean by the 'Kingdom of God'?"

"The Kingdom is within us when we accept Christ as our Lord and Savior. God becomes our King and the Ruler of our lives in everything we do or say. It's an eternal Kingdom. Are you a Christian, Allison?"

"Of course I am. My parents were Christians, and I've gone to church all my life."

"Have you accepted Jesus as your personal Savior?"

"I think so. I try to be as good as I can."

"Do you know for sure that if you died today you would go to heaven?"

"Can anyone know for sure? Only God knows if we are good enough for heaven."

"Would it surprise you to know that no one is good enough for heaven? We are all sinners and not fit for a Holy God. He sent Jesus to die on the cross as a sacrifice for our sins. It's only through the shedding of His blood that we can become good enough for God. His blood blots out our sins."

"What must I do to become a Christian, then?"

"God's gift of salvation is freely given through Christ, and all you have to do is accept it by faith."

"How do I do that?"

"Ask for forgiveness of your sins, turn from them, and commit your life to Him. If you are sincere, the Holy Spirit will guide you, and help you to a more abundant life in Him. You will become a new person, and that is the new birth. Do you want to do that right now?"

"Oh, yes, I do. I want to have what you and the Sullivans and the Ashleys have. I need peace of mind."

He took both of her hands in his and said, "We'll bow our heads, and you say what is in your heart to God."

Allison bowed her head and was quiet for a few minutes, and then she said, "Dear Lord, I have sinned, and I need Your forgiveness. Today I am turning from my sins, and I want you to be my Lord and Savior. Thank You for saving me."

With tears in her eyes, she raised her head and saw answering tears in Doug's eyes.

"Thank you for showing me the way, Doug," she said quietly.

"I'm happy for you, Allison," he said.

When they returned to the Sullivan's house, Doug went in with her while she told them the good news of her salvation. They rejoiced with her, and Callie asked, "Are you gonna be baptized tonight, Allison?"

"I...I haven't thought of that," she said.

"Don't rush her, Callie," Meg said. "She may need time to consider that."

After Doug left, Callie took Corley out in the yard to play, and Allison went to her room. She got down on her knees and prayed, asking the Lord to help her know what to do. There were so many problems in her life to be settled. When she got up, she took out the box of letters from Brad, and read the last one. Then she removed the gold ring from her finger, kissed it, and put it on top of the letters. His picture was on the dresser. She picked it up and looked at his blue eyes, honey-colored hair and strong facial lines. Then she kissed it, and placed it back on the dresser. I'll never forget you, Brad, she thought, but I must get on with my life.

She went into the living-room where Meg and Joe sat reading, and asked, "Could I be baptized tonight?"

"Sure!" Joe said happily. "I'll call Brother Mark right now and then take you over to talk to him. I've already filled the baptistery for the little Vandenberg boy. He asked Jesus into his heart a few weeks ago, but just lately decided to be baptized."

"I'll call the Ashleys and see if they want to be there tonight," Meg said.

*****

There were more people at church that night than usual. Word had gotten around that there would be two baptisms. The Ashleys were there, and they smiled at Allison. Corley went to them immediately and crawled up into Mr. Ashley's lap, which pleased him greatly.

Doug sat with Allison, and when the invitation for membership in the church by salvation and baptism or by letter was given, he stepped out of the way for her to go to the front. The preacher made known Allison's decision and request for baptism, and it was greeted with hearty "Amens."

Little Van was baptized first, and then Allison stepped down into the warm baptismal waters. Dressed in a white gown, she stood with her hands folded while Brother Mark said, "Allison, I baptize thee in the name of the Father and of the Son and of the Holy Spirit." As he put her under the water, he said, "Buried with Christ in baptism," and as she came up out of the waters he said, "and raised to walk in the newness of life." A peace came over her as she left the baptistry.

When she came out of the dressing-room, Doug was waiting for her. "I told the others if they wanted to take Corley home, I would bring you," he said.

He didn't say much on the way to the Sullivan's house, but when they got there he said, "I see you aren't wearing your gold band."

"I decided to put my old life behind me and start anew," she said.

He got out and opened the car door for her and walked her to the front door. When they reached it, he took her in his arms.

"Allison," he whispered hoarsely.

She looked up in surprise and saw the desire in his eyes. His lips came down on hers and lingered there for several seconds. The gentle kiss sent thrills through her body. He released her and walked back to his car and drove away, leaving her shaken and clinging to the doorknob.

Chapter XX

Ned Sutton was excited, but the only emotion he showed was a raising of the eyebrows and a twitch in his right cheek. His quarry had finally shown up. Two days he had been in this one room, rifle ready, staring at the large white house across the street and down one.

He had stopped at a service station on the outskirts of Oak Grove and borrowed the phone book. After he found the Ashley name, he wrote down the address. In the convenience store section of the station he bought a box of crackers, a package of cheese slices, a carton of Cokes, and two packages of cookies. Next he drove around until he found the street and house number. Luck was with him. Across the street on a house needing a coat of paint was a discreet sign that read "ROOM TO LET."

Mrs. Gatz, the owner of the house, was a garrulous elderly lady, and he paid her a week in advance. She had offered meals for a few dollars more, but he had declined. With one of his hard stares, he had discouraged her from hanging around talking.

The room was just where he wanted it, upstairs facing the street. There was a private bath and a small refrigerator. He noticed Mrs. Gatz took the sign down. It must be her only rental room. Perfect!

He thought about the woman that he would kill. How he hated her. She should have kept her mouth shut about what she had seen. It caused trouble for him. But he hated all women. Although he was indifferent about killing men, it was a pleasure to kill women. They were all liars and cheats like his mother had been. Still, he only did it for money. Killing was his way of making a living. This woman had witnessed the murder of that no good cop. She definitely had to go.

For two days no one had gone in or out of the house across the street except the elderly couple who lived there, but a maroon Mustang had just driven into the driveway.

His finger was poised on the trigger and his eye looked through the telescopic sight. When the tall black-haired woman got out of the car, she opened the back door, leaned in, and brought out a small child. At the same time, the door of the house opened and the couple came out. She put the toddler on the ground, and he ran to the old man. The women went into the house first, and the man and child followed, blocking his aim. All he could do now was to wait until she came out.

He stood up, stretched, walked over to the small refrigerator, and took out a Coke. When he went back to the window, he couldn't believe his luck. The young woman had come out of the house alone and was walking down the sidewalk toward him. Picking up his rifle, he took careful aim, and let out a curse word. A green Buick was blocking the view in his telescopic sight. Impatiently, he waited for it to move on, but when it did, the girl was gone! She had left in the Buick!

Cursing, he quickly put the safety on the gun and, carrying it, ran out of the room and down the stairs, intending to follow in his car. A small hand vacuum had been left on one of the steps, and he tripped over it and fell the rest of the way to the bottom. Mrs. Gatz came running out of the living-room, wringing her hands and apologizing. He was stunned at first, and then lay there moving his arms and legs, trying to assess if any bones were broken. Even though the pain was excruciating, he managed to sit up. All the time Mrs. Gatz hovered over him, crying and asking if he were all right, and if she should call a doctor or an ambulance.

"Get out and leave me alone!" he shouted, and she scurried back into the living-room.

His whole body ached, but he had learned to deal with discomfort years ago. He slowly stood up, slung the rifle strap over his shoulder, caught hold of the banister, and painfully pulled himself up the stairs. In his room he limped over to his bed and collapsed on the firm mattress, with the rifle lying across his chest. He would rest and then return to his vigil at the window. He hurt all over.

Memories of the pain he had suffered in childhood flooded his mind. His mother, dissipated by alcohol, cuffed him about whenever she felt like it. When a man spent the night with her, she sent Ned outside to sleep on the streets. It didn't matter to her if it was raining or snowing. If he dawdled, not wanting to go out in bad weather, the man would literally kick him out. Eventually he found a gang of boys who accepted him, and a warm shelter to live in. He never went back to his mother's room again. Later he learned that she had been killed by one of her men friends. No one claimed her body and he didn't care.

Finally he dozed off, and when he awoke it was dark. Cursing, he pulled himself out of bed and over to the window. The maroon Mustang was gone!

Chapter XXI

When Allison left the Ashley house, her mind was in a turmoil. As she hadn't slept well the night before, she told the Ashleys she needed fresh air. Doug's kiss had exhilarated her. It had been years since she had been kissed like that by anyone other than Brad. Did she love Doug? Over the past few weeks she had changed her first opinion of him from active dislike to friendship. Now she wondered if her feelings for him were the first twinges of love.

When he stopped by and asked her to go with him on a trip to see a patient in the country, she didn't hesitate. A feeling of happiness stole over her at the sight of him, and she wondered why she had been so restless and full of uncertainties about how she felt the night before.

They drove up into the hills, and when she saw the beauty all around her, she thought of God. The decision she had made to trust Him and follow the teachings of Jesus gladdened her heart. All the doubts and fears of the past few weeks were swept away. Just as the greening around her denoted a new birth in nature, so had she been reborn and was safe, sheltered under the wings of God.

"A penny for your thoughts," Doug said.

"I was marveling at the beauty of nature, and how my life has been changed," she replied.

He glanced at her and said, "You are happy, aren't you?"

With a smile, she said, "Yes, very happy."

"I noticed that you are calm. Not nervous like you were."

"Was it so obvious?"

"'Fraid so," he replied. "Here we are."

They had pulled up to a little shack among the trees. A few chickens were scratching around in the ground for worms, and in a nearby pen two pigs were wallowing in a mud puddle. A milk cow in a small cleared pasture lifted her head briefly and then went back to grazing. Next to the shack stood an ancient Ford pickup.

A small gray-haired woman, wearing a faded but clean cotton dress, came to the door to greet them. She had a puzzled look on her face.

"Hello, Dr. Doug," she said. "We weren't expecting you, but come on in. You, too, Miss. There are biscuits bakin' in the oven. I'll just put on a little pot of coffee, and we can have it with the biscuits and some blackberry jelly."

"You don't need to go to all of that trouble, Mrs. Kelly," Doug said. "I came by to see how Delbert is doing. Mr. Glass said he hasn't renewed his prescriptions, so I brought them along. He shouldn't be without his medicine, you know."

Mrs. Kelly didn't look up as she carefully measured the coffee, but said in a muffled voice, "I know, Doc, but we haven't been able to get to town. He isn't doing too well, either."

"Is he in bed?" Doug asked.

She nodded her head, and Doug took his black bag with him into the other room.

"Sit down, Miss," Mrs. Kelly invited, looking at Allison with bright blue eyes. "You sure are purty. Are you Doc's nurse?"

"No, my name is Allison Ames, and I'm a friend of his. I came along for the ride. The countryside is beautiful this time of year."

"Yeah, it be that, all right." She took the batch of biscuits out of the oven.

Allison noticed that although the room was sparsely furnished, it was neat and clean.

When Doug came back into the kitchen, he said, "His chest was filled with fluid. I gave him an I.V. dose of Lasix, and he should be okay now. Go ahead and start his medication, and don't neglect it again."

"I won't, Doc. Now you sit here. The coffee's ready, and I've put the biscuits, butter, and jelly on the table," she said, and began pouring the coffee into mugs. She sat down to drink a cup with them.

Fresh out of the oven, the biscuits were light and fluffy, and the soft yellow home-made butter melted on them. Allison helped herself to two of them and added blackberry jelly.

"This is delicious," she said, and her hostess beamed at the praise. Before they left, Mrs. Kelly brought out a dozen eggs in a small basket and gave them to Doug. "We don't have any cash money right now, but you take these eggs, and I'll pay the rest when I can," she said.

"Don't worry about that," Doug said. "Good fresh eggs are worth more than money to me."

"Goodbye," Allison said. "Glad to have met you, and thanks again for the coffee and biscuits."

Mrs. Kelly stood in the yard, waving until they were out of sight.

"That was a nice thing you did," Allison said with a look of admiration in her eyes.

"They're poor, but worthy people. Someone needs to look after them."

After they had driven a few miles down the country lane, Doug turned off onto another path that was even less traveled. It ended at the edge of a cliff overlooking the picturesque little town of Oak Grove, nestled in a curve of the Poteau River and surrounded by tall oak trees.

"How do you like our town?" Doug asked.

"Very much. It's beautiful there in the valley, with the green hills all around, and the people are all friendly. Almost seems as if it's in another time zone."

"That's the way I feel about it," he said. "It was a wonderful place to live as a child. Long, lazy, barefoot days of summer, fishing and swimming in the river, hunting and berry-picking in the woods. We played baseball, volleyball, and tennis but not organized sports like today. A group would just get together and play. When it was too hot to do anything else, I sat outside under a shade tree and ate an apple while I read a book. How did you spend your summers?"

Allison laughed. "My summers were busy. Piano and ballet lessons, trips to museums, art shows, and the zoo. Dad took a month off from his office to travel, and we gradually covered most of the United States plus a little of Mexico and Canada. Disneyland was my favorite, along with the Grand Canyon and Niagara Falls. In my spare time I read also."

"I agree. Your summers were busy. We did go to Disneyland once. Went to California to see Sue and her family when her husband was stationed there one other time. What kind of books do you read?"

"Ever since I read *Jane Eyre*, I've liked historical romances. What do you read?"

"Any kind of action books, western or spy stories mostly. You mentioned art. Do you go for those crazy modern artists? I like art that looks real, mostly western scenes or ships in stormy seas."

"Any picture with pretty colors pleases me. Monet and Renoir are two of my favorite artists."

"Do you still play the piano and practice ballet?"

"The piano, yes, but I'm rusty on the ballet. Do you like ballet?"

"Yes, what little I've seen. I didn't have much free time to go to plays and musicals while I was in school in Oklahoma City. We have some put on here by local actors, like the one we saw the other evening, but no ballet."

"I thought the actors were very good."

"Yes, they were. I thoroughly enjoyed the play."

They were silent for a few minutes, and then Doug said, "I feel as if we have gotten better acquainted today. That's why I brought you here. Seems as if we haven't had much chance to talk to each other. Tell me about your family. Where you were born. Things like that."

Allison wasn't sure how much she wanted to reveal about her past so she said, "Tell me about yours first."

"Okay. I was born in the Wolfeton Hospital on January 28, 1938, the youngest of three children. Dr. Newberry was the one who delivered me. My sister Sue was twelve, and my brother Thad was four. Do you have any brothers or sisters?"

"No. I'm an only child."

"My father Jack is the postmaster for Oak Grove, and my mother Bess is a home-maker. Sue is married to Major Charles 'Sandy' Moore, an air force pilot stationed at Edwards Air Force Base in California. They have six children."

"I love children, but don't think I could handle six."

"Then you'll be relieved to know that my brother Thad and his wife Angie only have three. He's a CPA and works for a firm in Tulsa."

"Why did you decide to become a doctor?"

"At first I thought I wanted to be a teacher, maybe even a coach. I lettered in three sports in high school under Joe, and I always admired him. He was a hero in World War II."

"Joe was? I mean, he's such a kidder, I didn't think he ever had a serious thought. What branch was he in?"

"He was in the Marines and fought all through the Pacific Theater. This town considers him a hero because he rescued Meg's brother Bob off an island, right under the noses of the Japanese. Bob was a pilot, and his plane was shot down. He bailed out on a small island and fractured his leg. Some natives found him and sent word to an American base. Joe was at that base, and he volunteered to get him off the island. A PT boat took him there, and he brought Bob back. They ran into five Japanese soldiers who were sent to capture Bob, but Joe slipped around and killed four of them, while Bob shot one who stumbled onto his hiding place."

"That was brave. I see Joe in a different light now."

"Don't mention this to him. He was pretty torn up by the war, and he tries to forget it."

"Is that the reason Bob went to the Philippines to be a missionary doctor?"

"Yes, he saw the need there and wanted to help them."

"And did you see the need here?"

"Back to that question," he said with a laugh. "I liked the science courses in high school, and at the university, I really got into them. At first I thought I wanted to do research, but Dr. Newberry had me see patients with him when I was home on vacation, and, yes, like Bob, I saw the need."

Allison looked at him tenderly with appreciation in her eyes and took his hand in both of hers. "I'm glad you did. You saved my son's life, and I'll always be grateful to you for that."

Doug glanced down at her hands holding his hand. His face flushed and he glanced out of the window at the town again. Finally he looked at her and said, "I'm happy that I was there for him and for you. Now, tell me about yourself. Where were you born?"

Allison released his hand and said, "I was born in Chicago on July 22, 1945. My father Calvin Corley is in real estate, and my mother Anne was a home-maker, like your mother. Nothing much exciting happened—usual childhood diseases, broke my arm once. That's about it, until I went to college at the University of Illinois and met Brad."

"Was it love at first sight?" asked Doug softly.

Tears filled her eyes and she brushed them away, "Not exactly. We had a couple of classes together, and became friends, and then started dating." She searched in her purse for a tissue. Doug handed her his handkerchief and she dabbed at her eyes with it and then continued, "He graduated the year before I would have. We got married and he went to work in a chemical plant. I was going to finish college, but found that I was pregnant, and dropped out. Corley was born ten months after we married and Brad was so proud of him. We had a few months together as a family, for which I'm grateful."

She paused again and sat still, twisting the handkerchief. "Brad's draft number came up after we had been married a little over a year, and they sent him to officers' school for three months. Since his degree was in chemistry, they had him in charge of detonating bombs. When he had been there six months, a bomb exploded before they got to it, and everybody was killed."

"If this is painful for you to talk about, you don't have to finish," Doug said.

"I need to tell you how it was. I was so much in love that it was difficult to be separated from him. Fear was my constant companion, and I was devastated when he was killed. Six months later my mother had a stroke and lingered for four months before she died. It was almost more than I could bear."

Doug put his arm around her and let her cry on his shoulder. "I didn't mean to upset you by bringing up the past," he said.

She quietly blew her nose in his handkerchief. "Talking about it is helping me put it behind me."

Her head rested on Doug's shoulder for a few minutes, and then she straightened up and drew away from him. "I didn't mean to be so weepy and mess up your hanky and your shirt. You must think I'm an emotional wreck."

"I'm just glad that I was here for you."

They sat in silence for a few minutes, and then Doug asked, "Your mother was a friend of Meg's?"

"No, they never met," she said. "I was adopted. It was my birth mother that Meg knew."

He looked at her seriously and asked, "Was Meg your birth mother?"

"No. She really was Meg's friend."

"In Oklahoma City?"

Allison decided to tell him the truth, so she said, "Yes, and here too."

Doug stiffened and sat very still. His face paled. In a tight voice he asked, "Is it my sister, Sue?"

"Oh, no!" she said, placing her hand on his. "My birth mother was Sylvia Ashley."

"Thank the Lord!" he said with relief. "For a moment I had the terrible feeling I was in love with my own niece."

Allison's heart gave a lurch. "What did you say?" she asked, with an astonished expression on her face.

He looked contrite. "I didn't mean to blurt it out that way." He took both of her hands in his and said, "I know it's too soon for you to think about loving another man, but I love you and I can't help it. When you think you can love again, keep me in mind. Now I had better get you back to the Ashleys. Have you told them yet?"

She looked down and picked some imaginary lint from her trouser leg. "Not yet," she said in a low voice.

"Why not? They're crazy about you and Corley, and I'm sure they'll gladly accept you as a granddaughter."

"It's—it's not the right time."

"When will it be the right time?"

"I don't know. Take me back. I've been gone long enough."

Doug looked into her worried face. "I know something is wrong. I wish you would trust me enough to tell me."

"Let me think it over and pray about it."

"I'll pray for you and for whatever is bothering you," he said, and backed the car, turned it around, and headed for town. They didn't talk much on the way. Both were busy with their own thoughts.

Chapter XXII

When he saw the Mustang was gone, Ned Sutton went back to bed. It was just as well. If he shot her now, he would be too sore to get out of there in a hurry. She would probably go there again. Meanwhile, he would rest, exercise, and get the soreness out of his body. Couldn't wait too long. Sylvia Ashley's lawyers could find her file was missing at any time. All he needed was the address and he would have put the file back, but he had heard the guard unlock the hall door and saw his flashlight beam as he came through the first office. He only had time to shut the drawer quietly and go through the other door into another office, from which he escaped into the hall.

Later he looked through the file and found that this Sylvia Ashley had an illegitimate baby in 1945, and the Corley couple had adopted her. This woman, Allison Corley Ames, was no doubt that baby grown up and was probably wanting to find her birth mother. The only address was Oak Grove, Oklahoma, and so he had come here. Luck had been with him. He had found her!

His stomach growled, and he felt hungry. He would have to get up and get some crackers and cheese. How tired he was of that diet! A soft knock sounded on the door.

"Who is it?" he asked, picking up his rifle.

"I brought you some vegetable beef soup," Mrs. Gatz said in a timid voice.

He shoved the rifle under the covers and said, "Come in, the door's not locked."

She entered with a bowl of steaming soup and a plate of cornbread and butter.

His stomach and salivary glands responded to the smell of the soup.

"Thanks," he said as she set it down on the bedside table.

"It's the least I can do since I spoiled your hunting trip," she said. "I am so sorry it happened. I need to be more careful."

"You're right. I could sue you, you know."

Her face blanched with fear. "You wouldn't do that, would you?"

"Not unless it got around town and some ambulance-chasing lawyer got hold of me and talked me into it."

"I won't tell anyone," she said. "While you're laid up, I'll bring your meals to you. You won't have to pay for them."

After she left, he wolfed the food down and, smacking his lips, decided it would be okay. He needed the rest, and she was a good cook.

Too bad, but he'd have to kill her before he left.

Chapter XXIII

Most of the night Allison prayed and thought about her problems. It was bad enough to have to tell the Ashleys that she was the illegitimate child of the daughter they had thought perfect, but she was in a dilemma about the other matter. She felt she should tell the police she was a witness to a murder, but then she would see the cold eyes of the killer and be gripped by fear. One of the policemen was an informant. What if he should tell the killer where she could be found?

"Trust in the Lord. He will watch over you," she told herself. But she could not let go of her fear.

The warm rays of the sun enticed Allison outside the next morning. She and Corley weeded the garden and planted flower seeds. Her problems were forgotten as she spaded the ground and smelled the freshly-turned dirt. Corley enjoyed putting the seeds in the holes she dug.

When they finished, she bathed Corley, fed him, and put him in bed for a nap. While he slept, she ate and then showered and dressed to go shopping.

"Corley's asleep. Do you mind watching him while I go to town and get a few necessities?" she asked Meg.

"You go ahead. I'll be here for him."

"Can I get something for you?"

"If you go to the Dixie Emporium, I could use more blue thread. Just a minute and I'll get the one I'm using for you to match.

Allison drove her Mustang to town and parked on Main Street in front of the drugstore. Most of her purchases would be there, but she decided to go to the Dixie Emporium first and get the thread for Meg. She window-shopped as she moved leisurely down the sidewalk. The western sun threw her shadow ahead of her. A beautiful green print dress caught her eye in the Dixie Emporium window and she stopped to admire it. Suddenly, she felt a presence behind her. She glanced ahead and saw the shadow of a tall man looming over her! He held an object in his raised hand. An icy draft traveled down her spine as she stared in horror. Stifling a scream, she whirled around to face him. It was Mr. Gregory, Doug's father. He was in his postal uniform and his cap was in his hand.

"I didn't mean to frighten you, Mrs. Ames," he said. Concern was written all over his face, and she knew that he must have seen the terror in her eyes.

Her mind searched for an excuse for her fear, but none came. Finally she blurted out, "That's okay. I was just admiring that dress and didn't hear you coming. When I saw your shadow, it startled me."

"Could I buy you a Coke or a cup of coffee?"

"Oh, that isn't necessary. I'm alright."

"I'd appreciate it if you'd let me."

She had the feeling that he really wanted to talk to her, so she agreed.

He escorted her into the Main Street Café. Several men were there drinking coffee, and they greeted him jovially. Although they tried to hide their curiosity, they looked surprised to see Allison with him.

Mr. Gregory led her over to a booth by the window. After they were seated, a waitress came to get their order.

"What will you have, Mrs. Ames?" Mr. Gregory asked.

"Coffee, please," she told the waitress.

"I'll have the same," he said.

After she left to get the coffee, Allison said, "Please call me Allison."

"Okay," he said, but he didn't ask her to call him Jack.

Nothing more was said until the waitress brought their coffee. Allison wondered why he wanted to talk to her. Could it be because Doug spent so much time in her company? She felt that he had planned to approach her when he saw her on Main Street. Stirring cream and sugar in her coffee, she waited for him to speak.

"I understand that you came from Chicago to visit Meg Sullivan?" It was more of a statement than a question.

"Yes," Allison said.

He cleared his throat and then said, "Your mother and Meg were friends?"

"Yes." She wasn't going to help him, and he sensed it.

"Did my daughter Sue know your mother?"

"I believe she did."

"In the Air Force, Sue gets acquainted with lots of people." Allison sat quietly sipping her coffee.

He took a sip of coffee and carefully set his cup down.

"I didn't know that Meg knew anyone in Chicago, except Sylvia Ashley, of course. Is that where she met your mother?"

"No, it was in Oklahoma City. My mother moved to Chicago during the war."

"Does she still live there?"

"She died a few months ago and my father is on a Mediterranean cruise. I was at loose ends, so I thought I'd look up my mother's old friend, Meg Sullivan." Allison didn't want to lie to him, but she couldn't reveal her kinship to the Ashleys before she told them. If they didn't accept her, she would quietly leave Oak Grove and no one would be the wiser.

"I'm sorry," he said. "You lost your husband recently, too. You've had your share of sadness. My wife and I would like for you to come to Sunday dinner with us sometime soon."

Allison was touched. "I'd like that." she said.

"Do you plan to be in Oak Grove very long?" He looked at her anxiously.

He's afraid I'm just amusing myself with his son, she thought. Doug's parents don't want to see him hurt, but I'm not sure how this will all turn out. Finally she answered him and said that she wasn't sure how long she would be here. "My father is due home in another month and I need to get back to Chicago to meet his plane," she said.

*****

Wednesday night she pleaded a headache and stayed home from prayer meeting. She felt as if she couldn't face Doug yet. Should she tell Meg and Joe about the murder and leave it up to them to tell the police, or confess to Doug first? By Friday she felt a strong desire to see Doug again, so she called his office and left word for him to call her.

When he called a few minutes later, he was concerned and asked, "Do you still have a headache?"

"I need to see you. Could you come by when you're through this afternoon, or could I meet you at your office?" she asked.

"I'll come by," he said.

She found Meg working in the garden.

"Would you watch Corley for me this evening? Doug is coming for me. I may have him take me to the Ashleys to tell them of my relationship to them."

"Of course I will. I'm relieved that you're going to tell them because I think they should know. Be sure and take the pictures Sylvia gave me and the letter she wrote to you. Don't worry. They'll be glad after the initial shock. I'll pray for you while you're gone.

"Thank you, Meg. There's something else I need to tell you, but I'll do this first."

Next she called the Ashleys and asked them if they were going to be home in the evening. They said they would be, and would welcome a visit from her and Corley.

"Doug is bringing me over first, and I'll bring Corley later."

Chapter XXIV

In Chicago on that same Friday morning, Dot Pierce drove her black Chevrolet into the parking garage next to her office building. She shuddered. A murder had been committed here a few weeks ago, and she thought about it every time she entered the garage. If it were not for the fact that it was conveniently close, she would have found another one.

As usual she was the first one to arrive at the office, and she pulled her key out of her purse and unlocked the door. When her husband died twenty years ago, she went to work as the receptionist for the lawyers Connel and Estes. Her desk was the first one inside the door and it was always neat and orderly. The calendar and the pencil holder, filled with sharpened pencils and capped pens, were placed in a certain place on the desktop, and she could tell if they had been moved so much as a sixteenth of an inch. It was the same with the drawers and their contents. She opened the top drawer on the right, took out the appointment book and opened it to the present date. One day last week she had thought this book was not quite the way she had left it, but when she mentioned it, no one took her seriously.

With a list of the clients who had appointments for that day, she went into the record room for their files. The first name on the list was Ashcroft. When she pulled this file out, she noticed the one behind it was missing. It was Sylvia Ashley's file. Hurriedly she checked through that drawer and came up empty-handed. Then she looked through all of the files, but couldn't find it. Mr. Estes arrived while she was searching, and she followed him into his office to report the missing file.

"I thought my log book had been moved last week," she said. "No one believed me, though."

*****

Gil MacDonald sat in his office, staring at the picture of the missing witness and wondering about her. She was beautiful, if the drawing was to be believed. Where could she be? Was she in danger? He ran his fingers over his hair and hoped she wasn't.

His daughter would probably have been about her age if she had lived. She had been the darling of his heart, and when she had died of leukemia at the age of six, his world had crashed around him. He had thrown himself into his work and stayed away long hours from home, leaving his wife to cope with her grief alone. Finally she couldn't take it anymore and had left him.

The phone rang. It was Captain Schumaker. "Mac, we just received a call from those lawyers, Connel and Estes. Someone broke into their office and a file is missing. It's the one we need to help us find the missing witness. Get over there pronto. We're sending a crew to get fingerprints and any other clues that will lead to the one responsible. We have a good idea who it is and don't really expect he left his prints. The woman's name is Allison Corley Ames. Officers have been sent to her apartment and to her father's house in Evanston."

Mac went immediately to the lawyers' office and questioned them about the woman. There were no fingerprints found except those of the office personnel. While he was there he received a call from the officers sent to her apartment. They reported that, according to her neighbors, she hadn't been there for a couple of months. The ones checking in Evanston called in with the same results.

"She could be in Oak Grove, Oklahoma," Mr. Estes volunteered. "That's where her natural grandparents, the Ashleys, live."

When Mac returned to the police station, he called the chief of police, Jay Bundy, in Oak Grove and asked him if Allison Ames was in town.

"Yeah, she's here," Chief Bundy replied. "What do you want with her?"

"Don't do anything until I get there, and I'll tell you then. Is there a small airfield near you?"

Chief Bundy gave him the name and location of the field.

"Have someone meet me there at around four," he said.

*****

When Doug drove up at five p.m., Allison was ready to go. She kissed Corley goodbye and hugged Meg before she left.

"What's this all about?" Doug asked as they drove down the hill toward town.

"I want you to convince me again that I should tell the Ashleys that I'm their daughter's illegitimate child," she said as she looked straight ahead.

He turned his head to look at her. "Allison, you know you should."

"Well, then, take me over there and let's get it over with," she said with a sigh.

"Good for you. Now what's the other problem?"

She looked at him, surprised. "How do you know there is another problem?"

"Allison, I know that there's something that has you scared. You ran away from Chicago because of it, didn't you?"

"Wh...what makes you think so?" she asked in a low voice.

"Aside from the fact that you've been nervous and jumpy, your neglect of Corley's illness was not normal for you. I've been around you long enough to know that you're a good mother, and it had to be pretty bad for you to drag a sick child around for two days without seeking medical attention."

Tears came to Allison's eyes and ran unheeded down her cheeks. Doug glanced at her, pulled over to the side of the road, and gently wiped her face with his handkerchief. He took her in his arms and kissed her on the forehead. She leaned against his shoulder and felt protected.

"I was going to tell you and the Sullivans after I got the ordeal with the Ashleys over," she said. "But I do need to tell someone. It's tearing me to pieces." She took his handkerchief and blew her nose. Then she poured out the whole terrifying story of the murder she witnessed and the fact that they had "ears" in the police department.

"I packed our clothes, picked up Corley, and fled," she said. "Before I left town, I called the police station, and gave them the license number of the murderers' car. Since then, I've been scared that somehow the killer would be able to track me down. Some nights I have bad dreams and see his evil face. I'll never forget it."

"My poor darling," he said holding her close. "We must pray about this now." He bowed his head and prayed, "Father, we ask for your protection of Allison from this evil man. Give her the courage to be a witness against him so justice may be done. We will trust in you to protect her and keep her safe under your wings. In Christ's name, amen."

"Thank you, Doug," she said. "Under His wings! That's from the book of Psalms, isn't it? I won't be afraid. Whatever happens to me, I know that God is with me."

"Let's go to the Ashleys and tell them that they are not alone anymore. They have a new granddaughter and great-grandson, and then we'll go to the police station. We can call Meg and Joe to meet us there," he said.

Chapter XXV

Oak Grove High School's baseball team was on the diamond practising for their final game of the season. It was to be against their greatest rival, Wolfeton High, a much larger school. Although they had never beaten them, they had high hopes this year. They had won the conference championship in their division due mostly to the talent of their pitcher, Bill Bradford, a senior. Wolfeton was in a higher conference than Oak Grove, and they only competed because they were neighboring towns.

In the locker room after practice, Joe was giving the team a pep talk when he received a note that he had a telephone call. He dismissed the boys and went to the office. It was the chief of police, Jay Bundy.

"Hi, Chief, what have I done wrong now?" he asked.

"I want you to come to the station right away! And don't tell anyone, not even your wife. Got it?"

"No, but I'll be there."

All the way to the station, he racked his brain trying to think of something he had done, or hadn't done, that the chief would be so mysterious about.

The chief had always reminded Joe of a bulldog with his barrel chest, narrow hips, heavy jowls, and bulging brown eyes. He also had the tenacity of one. Although he was pushing sixty-five, there was a force about him that belied his age.

When Joe entered the police station, he saw an undistinguished-looking stranger in a business suit talking to the chief and two of his officers. The conversation broke off as they turned to look at him.

He paused and looked quizzically at them. "Am I interrupting something?" he asked.

"No, come on in," the chief said. "This is Detective Gil MacDonald from Chicago. He brought us a picture that we find very interesting. Show it to him, Mac."

"Have you ever seen this woman?" the detective asked as he put a black and white sketch of Allison in front of him.

Joe's expression didn't change as he stared at the picture.

"Well, have you?" Mac asked

"Why? What has she done?" Joe asked.

"Don't try to be cute, Joe," the chief said. "I've seen her around town myself, and she's staying at your house. Her name is Allison Ames."

"Tell me why you want her, and I'll help you all I can," Joe said.

"We think she is the only witness to the murder of an undercover cop in a parking garage in Chicago," Mac said.

Joe gave a low whistle of amazement.

"It happened nearly two months ago, and that's when she came here," Chief Bundy added.

"How do you know she witnessed the murder?" Joe asked.

"She called us on the phone and told us that she had seen a man shot in a parking garage. For some reason she wouldn't leave her name, but she gave the license number of the killers' car."

"Why do you think it was her, and why wouldn't she give her name?"

Mac looked down ruefully. "She may have heard them mention that they had an informant in the police station."

"What!" Joe exclaimed. "Tell me all of the facts."

"About 1:50 p.m. on March 30, a man went into the garage to get his parked car and discovered a body with a bullet hole in the middle of the forehead. It looked like a gang killing, and through our investigation we learned that the victim was an undercover policeman. He had infiltrated a Mafia gang and was a key witness against Dom Giovanni, an influential Mafia boss."

"And I suppose his cover was blown by the spy in your station," Joe said.

"Yes. This made us suspicious, so we set a trap for the rat, but not before he did more damage."

"What else did he do?" asked the chief.

"After we received the call from the woman, we started looking for her, and we got a description of the last woman to leave the garage from the ticket attendant. It seems he was quite impressed with her looks and remembered her in detail, and also her car, a maroon Mustang. He had watched her come and go from the building next to the garage. We had him come to the police station and help our artist draw her picture."

"Isn't it great what they can do nowadays?" Officer Jerry Adams asked as he looked at the likeness of Allison.

"We showed it to the security guards at the building that the boy had indicated and found that they remembered her. Apparently she is a strikingly beautiful woman."

"I'll say she is!" Sid, the other officer, said and then looked uncomfortable when Chief Bundy frowned at him.

Mac continued, "A young man passed by and glanced at the picture. He worked on the seventh floor and said that he saw her go into the offices of the lawyers, Connel and Estes. The lawyers wouldn't give us any information because of the confidentiality of lawyer-client relationship."

"What about the car license?" Joe asked. "Did you pick the guys up?"

"We got the owner of the car, Dom Giovanni, locked up. But Ned Sutton, his driver and hit man, got away."

"Got away!" Joe exclaimed. "How did that happen?"

"The snitch in our station warned him. Yesterday the lawyers of the firm where Allison had an appointment informed us that their offices were broken into, and the file of Sylvia Ashley from Oak Grove was gone. They don't know when it happened, except it was after we had inquired about it."

"How did he know which file to take?" Chief Bundy asked.

"The names, dates, and time of appointments are listed in a log on the receptionist's desk. He just had to turn to the date, check the hour to find out who was there just prior to the hour of the killing. Her name was listed on the roster as Allison Corley Ames-Ashley, and her appointment was at one p.m. Evidently he found her file under Ashley and took it. He put everything, except the file, back in place, like a professional thief."

"That means he could be here now waiting for a chance to kill Allison!" Joe exclaimed.

MacDonald looked glum. "There's more," he said.

"More! What do you mean—more?" Joe asked belligerently.

"A little over a week ago, the killer shot the detective who was feeding him all the information."

"I thought you had a trap set for him," Chief Bundy interjected.

"He was under surveillance, but somehow the killer got into his apartment at night and killed him. In the morning he was seen leaving, but he got away," Mac said.

"Joe, we want you to quietly bring Allison and her son here so we can place them in a safe house until we can pick up the hit man," the chief said. "We don't want to cause a panic in town, which could make the killer move faster."

"I'll go home and get them right now," Joe said.

When he arrived there he found Corley, but Allison was gone.

"Where's Allison?" he asked urgently.

"What's the matter, Joe?" Meg asked. "Doug has taken her to see the Ashleys, and she's going to tell them that she's Sylvia's daughter."

Joe hurried upstairs and came down with his hunting rifle.

When Meg saw the rifle, her face blanched. "What are you going to do, Joe? Please tell me what this is all about."

"Haven't got time." Rushing outside, he jumped into his pickup. He spun out of the driveway and down the graveled road in a cloud of dust.

"Callie, watch Corley. Sarah, watch the pot roast," Meg said. She picked up her purse and car keys, got in the station-wagon, and hurried after him.

*****

It had been nearly a week, and Ned was getting restless. Most of the soreness was gone, and he was able to spend a lot of time at the window. But there had been no sign of the maroon Mustang.

Mrs. Gatz was still bringing his meals to him. He always hid the rifle and got in bed when it was time for her to come. She brought the paper every day also, but it was local news. Who cared about what went on in Podunk, anyway? Most of the time he played solitaire and listened to the radio. It was hard to get any station except one, and it only played country music.

Today he was about ready to give up and go looking for her. Couldn't wait too much longer. The missing file could be noticed at any time, and the police would come swarming.

As he was ready to get back in bed for his supper, he saw the green Buick coming down the street. Sure enough it turned into the driveway of the Ashley house. He had his finger on the trigger and his eye on the telescopic sight when Mrs. Gatz knocked on his door.

"Mr. Jones, I have your supper."

"Not now!" he shouted.

The black-haired woman and a man got out of the car and walked the short distance to the front door. The door opened, and the man glanced over his shoulder at the window. Ned fired! They both fell in the doorway.

Mrs. Gatz screamed and dropped the tray when the loud report of the gun came from the bedroom. Ned dashed out, rifle in hand. He knocked her toward the stairs and shoved her. She felt herself falling and grabbed the banister. Rushing past her, he fled to his car parked in the alley behind the house and sped away.

*****

As Doug followed Allison into the house, he had caught a flash of light out of the corner of his eye. He turned his head and saw the western sun shining on the barrel of a rifle that was protruding from a window and pointing in their direction. Instinctively, he shoved Allison down and fell on top of her. The bullet whizzed over their heads and landed harmlessly in the wall of the entry way.

"What was that?" asked Mr. Ashley in shocked surprise. He had opened the door and stepped aside to let them in.

"Someone was shooting at us," Doug said. "Are you all right, Allison?"

"A little bruised," she said, as he helped her to her feet.

127

Doug cautiously peered out of the window and saw Mrs. Gatz come screaming out of her house. He ran out into the yard, and she pointed behind her house and yelled, "He ran out to his car in the alley!"

"Call the police, and I'll follow!" he shouted to Allison.

"No, Doug, stay here! He's a dangerous man and has a gun!" she cried, but he was already in his car, starting to back out the driveway.

*****

When Joe turned the corner and saw people running from their houses into their yards, he knew the killer had struck. A blue Dodge raced past up the street, but he had to see if Allison was okay first. He saw Doug getting into his car and Allison standing in the yard with Mrs. Ashley's arm around her. Stopping behind Doug's car, he told him to get in and then turned the pickup around and sped after the Dodge.

Mr. Ashley called the police, and immediately two squad cars pulled out of the station and joined the chase.

At the same time, Meg arrived in her station-wagon, and Allison tearfully told her the highlights of what had happened. Without any hesitation, Meg said that she was going to follow Joe. Allison got in the car with her, in spite of the objections of the Ashleys, and they rushed after the screaming sirens of the police cars.

The killer's car had a souped-up motor, and he quickly outdistanced the others, but he had lost his way and headed out of town on a lesser highway full of hills and curves.

Joe hadn't gone far when he abruptly swerved onto a narrow road that was little more than a pair of ruts.

"This is a short cut, and we can get ahead of him," he said. "It's bumpy and steep, so hang on!"

The police cars raced by, followed by Meg and Allison, but Joe and Doug were already out of sight on the little-used road.

After what seemed an eternity of bumps and curves, they finally came out on the highway. Joe rounded a hill and then parked the pickup in the middle of the road to block the fugitive. There was no way around. A steep hill was on one side, and a deep ravine on the other.

Joe picked up his rifle, and they climbed out of the pickup, just as the blue Dodge came careening around a hill, a mile down the road. When they saw that he wasn't going to stop, they started climbing the hill. Joe stepped on loose rock and slid back down, hurting his leg. Doug started back down to help him, but Joe yelled at him to stay there. He stood up and aimed his rifle at the Dodge. Suddenly a dead Japanese came rolling toward him in a tank, with his eyes wide open and blood running down his face. Joe's arm was paralyzed. He couldn't pull the trigger.

At that moment the two squad cars and the station-wagon came around the curve. The occupants witnessed the car hurtling toward the men and the pickup. They screeched to a halt.

Allison and Meg gasped and grabbed each other in fear for the men's safety.

The policemen in the squad cars looked on in horror.

"Joe! Joe!" Doug was sliding down the hillside. "Shoot!"

The Japanese soldier in the tank disappeared, and Joe looked into the sneering face of the driver speeding toward him. He took aim. Suddenly the killer's face was distorted by an expression of terror as he looked beyond them at something only he could see. He stomped on his brakes. They squealed. His car spun out of control, plunged over the side, and crashed into the ravine.

Then silence.

Doug and Joe stood in a daze. Doug was the first one to speak. "You didn't fire, did you?"

Joe shook his head. "No, I started to, but a terrified look came to his face, and he skidded out of control. I wonder what specter he saw from his past."

After the initial shock, Meg said, "Thank you, Lord!" and then both she and Allison hurried out of the station-wagon, ran past the policemen, and into the waiting arms of Joe and Doug.

"Good shooting, Joe," Chief Bundy said.

"I didn't shoot," Joe said.

"What happened then?" Mac asked.

"I don't know," Joe replied. "He got an expression of horror on his face, slammed on the brakes, and skidded over the side. I think something from his past loomed up and scared him."

"Naw, that man didn't have a conscience," Mac assured them. "He must have tried to stop to save his own hide."

"Take the women on home," Chief Bundy said. "We'll have the car and the driver's body brought up and examined. Tomorrow will be soon enough to get your statements."

"Maggie and I will take the pickup home and call the Ashleys," Joe told Doug, "and you bring Allison in the station-wagon."

"Come and eat supper with us, Doug," Meg said.

"After we eat, I'll take you to the Ashleys to get your car," Joe added.

On the way home, Allison began shaking so hard that Doug pulled over to the side of the road and took her in his arms. He kissed her gently on the forehead and said, "It's over, Allison. You don't have to fear that man anymore."

She gradually stopped trembling and settled down in his arms. Her head was pressed against his chest, and she could hear the strong, steady beat of his heart. Was this feeling she had for him love? Or was she just grateful that he had risked his life for her? Could another man ever take the place of Brad in her heart?

Finally Allison ceased trembling and Doug started the motor. They drove the rest of the way in silence.

When they reached the Sullivan's house, he took her in his arms and kissed her again before they went in.

"Here are your keys, Joe," he said, handing them to him.

"You're going to eat with us, aren't you, Doug?" Meg asked. "We're having a pot roast, potatoes, and carrots."

"Thanks, I believe I will," he said.

Both of the men ate with a good appetite, but the women only toyed with their food. Meg and Joe had briefly explained to the children what had happened and warned them not to mention it to Allison at this time.

After supper, Joe took Doug to get his car, and to explain to the Ashleys how this terrible thing came about.

"I'll tell them about the events that led up to this evening, but not the reason you were in the lawyer's office," Doug told Allison before they left.

That night in bed, Meg nestled in Joe's strong arms and said, "Joe, I was so afraid. I couldn't bear it if anything happened to you."

Joe was quiet for a few minutes and then said, "Maggie, I think the Lord intervened to keep me from killing that mad dog. I was ready to shoot when I had a vision of a dead Japanese soldier. It paralyzed me for a few seconds. Then the next time I aimed at the killer, his face twisted in a look of horror, and he stomped on the brakes and swerved off the road. He must have seen a ghost from his past, too. The Lord knew that I couldn't handle snuffing out another human life, even an evil one like that."

Meg pulled his head down and kissed him, and then said, "Poor Allison. She was terrified that he would find her. I knew she was worried, but she wouldn't confide in me."

"I'm glad she finally told Doug. They planned to inform the police and us after they told the Ashleys that she was their granddaughter."

"It's a shame that after all she has been through today, she still has to face them with the news that Sylvia had an illegitimate child."

Chapter XXVI

Allison tossed and turned in her bed that night. The whole terrible scene of the past evening kept replaying in her mind. Doug and Joe had risked their lives to catch the man trying to kill her! When she and Meg had come around the bend in the road and had seen the danger the men were in, she realized that she cared deeply for Doug, and if he were killed another light would be gone out of her life. But was it love?

Other thoughts came into her mind. She still had to tell the Ashleys who she was. If they rejected her, she couldn't stay in the same town with them. Before all of these terrible events had happened, she had enrolled in Northwestern University for the fall term. She had planned to give up her apartment and move in with her father in Evanston. That way she would be close to the university and could get her degree in Business Administration.

Did she love Doug? She knew he loved her and would soon ask her to marry him. But the town needed him. If she accepted him, it would be essential that the Ashleys acknowledge her as Sylvia's daughter. The more important it became, the more she dreaded telling them.

"Lord, help me," she prayed, and finally went to sleep.

The next morning when she woke up she heard Meg in the kitchen. Corley was still asleep, so she quietly slipped out of bed, put on her robe and slippers and went in to join her.

"You're just in time to drink a cup of coffee with me," Meg said and poured two cups.

Allison sat down at the breakfast table across from her, and said, "Meg, I want to ask a favor of you."

"What is it?"

"Will you go with me today to tell my grandparents that I'm Sylvia's daughter? You'll be able to explain the circumstances better than I."

"Sure, I'll go with you. They are morally strict, but they are good people, and I feel certain that they will forgive their daughter and accept you and Corley. However, let's wait until Sunday afternoon. Saturday is a busy day in their grocery store, and both will be working."

Around ten a.m., the chief called them to come to the police station to give their statements about the events of the day before. When they arrived Doug was there, as were Mrs. Gatz and the Ashleys.

After they had given their statements and discussed the matter from the time Ned shot his rifle to the crash, the chief told them that Ned Sutton died of massive injuries, including a broken neck.

"There were no bullet holes in him or the car," the chief said. "I wonder why he went over the side that way?"

"Guilty conscience," Joe said.

The chief snorted, "A man like that has no conscience."

"What causes a man to be like that?" Mrs. Ashley asked.

"He began young," Mac said. "Unloved and abused as a child, he was thrown out on the street at an early age. Started out stealing to get food and then got in with a gang. Reform school and later prison, just made him worse. With the Mafia he found his speciality---killing for hire."

"How awful!" Mrs. Gatz said. "I...I didn't know that. I thought he had come here to hunt with his rifle and all. He wasn't a friendly man. In fact I was afraid of him, but I never thought of him as a murderer. Who would suspect it in our town? It's all my fault." Tears came to her eyes, and she blew her nose.

Allison's heart went out to her and she put her arm around her, "No, Mrs. Gatz, if anyone is to blame, I am. I'm the one he was after."

"No one is responsible, except Ned Sutton himself," Mac said. "His whole life led up to that moment. He had to be stopped one way or another. I'm just glad that no one else was hurt."

"When he ran out of the room he tried to knock me down the stairs, but I caught hold of the banisters," Mrs. Gatz said, and shivered.

"If you're through with us," Mr. Ashley said, "the wife and I better get back to the store."

"I must go to the hospital and finish my rounds. See you later, Allison," Doug said and left.

"Would you and Corley come over tomorrow afternoon, Allison?" Mrs. Ashley asked.

"Yes, thank you. We will," she replied.

"I'm afraid that I need you to go back to Chicago with me tonight, Mrs. Ames," Mac said. "We'll need your personal testimony of the killing."

"Oh, no," Alison exclaimed. "Doesn't this horror ever end?"

Meg put her arm around her shoulders and said, "Leave Corley with us and then come back as soon as you're finished."

"I'm sorry to put you through this," Mac said. "It'll probably be evening before I'm finished here."

"Since tomorrow is Sunday, can't I wait until Monday? I have something important to do tomorrow."

"I'll tell you what. We'll leave early in the morning. I'm afraid we can't wait any longer. We need your statement before Dom Giovanni is released for lack of evidence."

"I'll be ready," she answered dully.

"Are you coming to the ball game this afternoon, Chief?" Joe asked.

"Wouldn't miss it," he replied.

*****

After lunch, Joe, Jimmy, and Sammy went to the ball diamond to get the field ready.

"We have to mark base lines and tie down the bases," Joe explained to Allison. "You and Corley are coming, aren't you?"

"Sure, we'll be there rooting for our team," she said.

"We'll have to go early to get a good seat," Meg told her. "There's great rivalry between the two teams, and nearly everyone in town will be there, plus half of Wolfeton."

Both women changed into jeans and cotton blouses. Allison pulled her hair back into a pony-tail, tying it with two ribbons, a blue one and a white one, to match the school colors.

When they arrived at 1:30, the stands were nearly full. Sammy had saved them seats behind home plate. As soon as they were seated, he left. "Gotta go help Dad," he said. "I'm a bat boy."

As they started to sit down, Allison noticed the Hunter family sitting behind them. She knew Joe and Meg had been helping Frank get work and encouraging them to attend church.

"Hello," she said. "Is Frankie playing on this team?"

Cora smiled shyly at her and nodded her head.

"Hi, Cora and Frank," Meg said. "And here are Becky and Betsy, and little Bryan. Is this your first game?"

The little girls nodded, and Frank said, "We thought we would come to see our boy play. Haven't been able to come before."

"Glad you could make it," Meg said. "Frankie is a good player."

"There's Kathy. I'm going to sit with her," Sarah said.

"Room for us?" asked a large blond man with a receding hairline. Behind him was a pretty woman with gray-streaked brown hair.

"Sure, have a seat," Meg said, and moved closer to Allison to make room for them. "Allison, meet Mel and Sally Bradford. You met their son, Bill, the other night when he came by to pick up Sarah."

"Yes, the star pitcher for our team," she said with a smile.

"I hope he's in good form," Sally said nervously. "Everyone is depending on him to help us beat Wolfeton for the first time."

"Joe isn't putting pressure on him," Meg said. "He keeps telling the boys that it takes all of them to win."

Corley was seated between Allison and Callie, and he took that moment to lean around Allison to say, "I little Corley."

"Well, hello, little Corley," Sally said. "Glad to meet you."

Mel leaned over and shook the small hand. "I bet you will be out there pitching one of these days," he said.

Meg thought it was a good time to introduce the Bradfords to the Hunter family, so she said, "Mel and Sally Bradford, meet Frank and Cora Hunter and their children, Betsy, Becky, and Bryan. Their son Frankie is on the team."

"Glad to meet you," Mel said. "Joe told me about you, Frank, and I've been meaning to get in touch. We need another man to work in the lumberyard. Would you be interested?"

"I shore would," he replied. "I've been wantin' a steady job."

"Good. Report to my office at the Bradford Lumber Company out on Highway 102, Monday morning at eight."

Before the game, several people came by to tell Allison they were glad she wasn't injured by the killer. They were curious and full of questions, and Meg helped her answer them. She was relieved when the game finally started.

It was a close game, hotly fought, with many cheers and jeers from the fans. Finally the last inning arrived with the score tied at four. Wolfeton batted first, and Bill Bradford was pitching. Only one run came in, but the opposing team was now ahead. Frankie, the first one to bat for Oak Grove, got a single and was cheered by the Oak Grove fans. The next batter also hit a single, and Frankie made it to second. Outs by the following two batters caused the fans to sigh. Bill Bradford walked, and the bases were loaded with two outs when Jimmy came up to bat. The Oak Grove fans groaned, and the Wolfeton fans cheered. He had struck out both times he had been up to bat before. Meg hurt for him. What did they expect from a freshman? She wished Joe had substituted a good hitter for him, though. But Joe would never do that because he felt every player should have his chance.

Jimmy swung hastily at the first ball and missed. He let the next two wild pitches pass, and then fouled the fourth. The fans on both sides were in an uproar. Another ball passed, and the umpire held up three fingers on his left hand and two on his right. Oak Grove fans cheered. Jimmy stepped out of the batter's box to wipe his sweaty palms on his pants. He looked at his father. Joe smiled and gave him a nod of encouragement.

When he stepped back in the box, the fans held their collective breaths. The Wolfeton pitcher wound up for the last pitch. A determined look was on Jimmy's face. He swung mightily at the fast ball coming toward him. The ball hit the bat with a loud crack. It sailed high into the air. An astonished expression crossed Jimmy's features. He threw down the bat and ran faster than he had ever run in his life.

The crowd went wild. The boys on third, second, first, and finally Jimmy came running over home plate. The game was over. Oak Grove had at last beaten the mighty Wolfeton team!

Two large Oak Grove players tossed Jimmy up on their shoulders and hauled him around the diamond. The rest of the players followed and the fans cheered.

Meg and Allison were laughing with joy and hugging each other. Mel and Sally shouted their congratulations to Meg over the noise.

"Now I know why you get nervous when Bill is pitching, and everyone is expecting him to win!" Meg yelled back.

Callie picked Corley up and danced around with him in her arms.

Sam and Alice Mitchell came by, and Sam said, "We're treating the team at the Freezer Queen. Want to go?"

"Can we, Mom?" Callie asked.

"Yes, you all go with Granddad, and I'll wait for Joe," she replied. "He may need me to take some of the boys in the station-wagon."

As they were getting in Sam's car, Doug drove up. "Game over?" he asked. "Who won?"

"We did," Sam said, and then they all tried to talk at once to tell him about Jimmy's home run.

"Sounds like an exciting game. Sorry I had to miss it."

"Want to go to the Freezer Queen for ice-cream?" Sam invited. "I'm buying."

"I'll pass this time," he said. "Allison, could I have a word with you before you go?"

"We'll wait," Sam told her.

Doug drew her aside and said, "Could I take you out to dinner tonight?"

Her heart gave a lurch. "Yes, what time?"

"I'll be by for you at six. Is that too early?"

"No. That's fine. I'll be ready."

Corley leaned out of the car window and said, "Hi, Dub."

Doug tousled his hair, and said, "Hi, Pardner."

Chapter XXVII

Promptly at six, Doug rang the doorbell at the Sullivan's house. He was dressed in his best gray suit with a white shirt and a maroon and gray tie.

"Come in," Joe invited as he opened the door. "I think she's about ready."

"I heard that you have a hero here," Doug said, smiling at Jimmy. Jimmy returned his smile and then ducked his head in embarrassment.

Allison came into the living-room wearing a two-piece rose-colored dress, pearl necklace, and matching pearl ear drops. Her shoulder-length black hair was softly curled at the ends, framing her beautiful face. Doug looked into her lovely brown eyes and his heart turned over.

"Take good care of her and have her home by midnight," Joe said jokingly.

"The Oxford Hotel in Wolfeton has a new restaurant named the Amber Room," Doug said as he drove down the winding road from Blueberry Hill. "I have reservations there for seven."

"Do you think they'll allow us in Wolfeton tonight?" Allison teased.

Doug grinned. "If we're quiet, maybe they won't suspect we're from Oak Grove."

The town of Wolfeton, like Oak Grove, was crowded on Saturday night. The stores stayed open late for the shoppers' convenience, and a line was forming outside the movie theater.

Doug parked in the hotel parking-lot, and they entered the elegant lobby. A few guests were taking advantage of the golden-velvet settees scattered around the area. The plush amber rug was springy under their feet as they crossed to the dining-room entrance. Doug gave his name to the hostess at the door of the dining-room. She looked at the ledger on the lectern and then signaled a waiter to seat them. They were led to a table in a quiet corner. A woman in a saffron dress was playing quietly on a baby grand piano. Golden brocade drapes hung at the tall windows. Amber glass surrounded the lights in the wall sconces, casting a golden glow over the room. A crystal vase with a deep yellow rose stood in the center of each white damask-covered table.

"This is nice," Allison said.

"It's uptown dining for sure," Doug agreed.

The waiter gave them each a menu and filled the crystal goblets with water. "What would you like to drink?" he asked.

"Iced tea, please," Allison said.

"I'll have the same," Doug added.

Allison glanced at Doug and thought him handsome and distinguished in his gray suit. He raised his gray eyes from the menu and looked into her brown ones, and her heart fluttered. At that moment a waitress came to take their orders.

While they ate their salads they talked about everything except what was uppermost in both their minds. Allison suspected he was planning to ask her to marry him, but she still wasn't sure if she was ready.

"When do you expect your father to return?" Doug asked.

"In a couple of weeks," she replied.

"Is your father retired?"

"No, but he owns a real estate business and has always been able to take off whenever he desires."

"Do you live with him?"

"I have an apartment in Chicago, but my lease expires this month, and I plan to move in with him. I've already enrolled in Northwestern University at Evanston to finish my last year and get my degree. You've been popping in and out of my life the past few weeks, but I don't even know where you live. Do you live with your parents?"

"No. I live in an apartment over our offices," he said and laughed. "It's strange that we don't know much about each other, yet I feel as if I know you well."

After dinner, Doug drove to the Wolfeton Park. "Would you like to walk?" he asked. "The parks are safe here."

A full moon, shining through the leafy branches of trees, traced a black and silver pattern over the path as they walked. Not many people were in the park—a man exercising his dog, and a few couples strolling or sitting on benches.

"I've been in this park at night before," Allison said.

"Oh, you have?" Doug asked, surprised.

"Yes. One evening when Corley was in the hospital and was so cross and feverish, I was at my wits end. I hadn't eaten all day, and I was worried sick. Joe and Meg came up to help me. I didn't think I could eat a bite, but Meg stayed with Corley while Joe made me go with him to eat. Instead of eating in the hospital cafeteria, he took me to the Black Cat Café. I was hungrier than I realized and ate ravenously."

"Poor Allison. I was too harsh with you," Doug remembered. "I didn't realize what a strain you were under. I'm glad they were kind and made up for my rudeness."

"You were worried about Corley, and you were right. I should have stopped and had him taken care of sooner."

"That was no excuse for my rough treatment of you. Joe and Meg are exceptional people. They always seem to know what people need and try to help them. Joe is a great coach, too. He's had offers to go to larger schools with a higher salary, but he turns them down. He and Meg are content to take it easy and live in this small town."

"They love this town and their house on Blueberry Hill. The hill has fond memories for them. Meg told me that that is where he proposed to her."

"I know, but I didn't bring you here to talk about Joe. How are you handling this past bad experience?"

"I'm relieved that I don't have to worry about that killer. But Detective MacDonald needs me to give my testimony about the murder I witnessed. Dom Giovanni stayed in the shadows, so I can't identify him for certain, but I did see the car tag. He wants me to fly back with him tomorrow morning."

Doug raised his eyebrows in surprise. "Will you have time to talk to the Ashleys before you leave?"

"No. That's the bad part. I hate putting it off. It's just one more problem to think about. While I'm there, I'm going to Evanston to get my father's house ready before I meet him at the airport."

Doug led her to a bench, and they sat down. He drew her in his arms and kissed her hungrily on the lips. In spite of her firm resolve, she responded with equal passion.

"Allison," he asked huskily, "will you marry me."

She stiffened and withdrew slightly. He had caught her by surprise. She wasn't expecting him to ask her without building up to it. But, that was his way—blunt and direct.

"I-I need more time, Doug. So much has happened lately. I like you a lot, but I need to think about it. Also, I still have to tell the Ashleys that I'm Sylvia's daughter. If they don't accept me, I'll have to leave this town."

"I know they'll welcome you. Look how crazy they are about you and Corley. But if they don't, I'll go anywhere with you—even to Chicago."

"The people need you so much here that I couldn't ask you to leave. Let me sort my feelings out while I'm in Chicago."

"I've waited years for you to come into my life. A few more days won't make that much difference," He took her in his arms and kissed her again. "Allison, I have prayed for the Lord's will ever since I felt myself falling in love with you. When you accepted Jesus as your Savior, I knew it was a sign from God that you were the one He had in mind for me. You're the first woman that I have wanted to spend my life with, and this is why I'm certain the Ashleys will acknowledge you."

Allison was touched by this declaration by Doug. She knew he was a deeply sincere, but cautious, man who wouldn't jump into anything without strong convictions. "Thank you, Doug," she whispered. "I...I just need more time."

*****

Corley was in bed asleep when Allison returned to the house on Blueberry Hill. Joe and Meg were reading in the living-room and looked up expectantly when she walked in.

"Thank you for watching Corley," she said. "I need to pack tonight. Are you sure you don't mind taking care of him while I'm gone?"

"We're glad to. He's no trouble at all. Mrs. Ashley said she would keep him on the days I teach school," Meg reassured her.

Allison tossed and turned in bed that night. It worried her that she had to testify against Dom Giovanni. His dark figure loomed over her like a bad omen. Would he hire other hit men to come after her? She slipped out of bed and fell to her knees. "Father, I love you and I'm trusting you to protect me from that man. Please keep me safe under Your wings. Give me peace of mind, I beg You."

She crawled back into bed, closed her eyes and went to sleep.

Chapter XXVIII

About one p.m., Sunday afternoon, the plane carrying Allison and Detective MacDonald arrived at O'Hare in Chicago. A detective in an unmarked police car met them. Allison had thought about renting a car, but the detectives decided it would be safer for them to take her home.

When they reached her apartment, Allison started to get out of the car, but Detective MacDonald stopped her.

"Let me go in first and search it," he said. After a thorough inspection, he came back and said it was okay. He carried her bag in for her and said that they would pick her up at nine a.m. Monday, and take her to the police station.

After they left, Allison pulled the drapes back from the large picture window that faced Lake Michigan and gazed at the sparkling waters. She would miss this view when she gave up this apartment on Lake Shore Drive.

With the sunlight shining through the windows, she noticed how thick the dust had become in her apartment. She spent the next hour sweeping and dusting. After she finished she thought of her friend Elna Evans. Elna was a writer and did her work at home on her electric typewriter. I'd better give her a call, she thought.

Elna answered the phone and when she recognized Allison's voice she said, "Where have you been and how is Corley? After I dialed your number several times and didn't get an answer, I called all of the hospitals to see if he had been admitted to one of them."

"I'm so sorry I didn't let you know where we were. Corley had pneumonia, but he's well now. Could I meet you for lunch tomorrow? I'll tell you all about my adventures."

"I'd like that. Where do you want to eat?"

"How about our old favorite place, Maude's Tea Room?"

"Sure, what time?"

"Is one o'clock okay?"

"Yeah, I'll be there. I can't wait to hear what you have to say. It better be good!"

*****

The next morning, a detective picked up Allison and took her to the police station. She spoke into a recorder and told everything about the murder she had witnessed. They asked her many questions and when they were satisfied with her testimony, they offered to take her back to her apartment.

Since it was only eleven a.m. she said, "No thanks. I intend to do some shopping and then meet a friend for lunch."

Her favorite stores were nearby and she needed to purchase some cosmetics. As she sauntered down the sidewalk she stopped to look in the different shop windows. It felt good to be back in Chicago. Would she miss the hustle and bustle of the big city if she married Doug and made Oak Grove her permanent residence? Why think of that. She wasn't sure her love for him was that strong. Thoughts of her great love for Brad interfered. She had put her wedding band back on this morning. Suddenly an eerie feeling came over her. Was she being watched? She glanced over her shoulder slowly, afraid of what she would see. No one in particular was noticing her. Still she couldn't shake the fear. A little later she spun around, but everyone behind her seemed intent on their own business. My imagination is working overtime, she thought.

She entered Marshall Field's Department Store and approached the cosmetic counter where she looked over the display. After she made her purchases, she strolled through several aisles admiring the merchandise. Time ran out and she didn't have time to try on clothes, but maybe she could get Elna to shop with her the next day. In the clothing department she stopped to feel the fabric of different dresses. This reminded her of her mother. One day after she had been shopping, her mother said, "Well, did you buy anything or did you just look and feel?" Thinking about that brought memories of her mother. How she missed her! Her mother had suffered so much the last few days of her life that death had been a release.

In the lingerie department she found a beautiful filmy green nightgown with a matching peignoir. Buying something new was just the thing to make her feel good about herself. She turned around with it in her hands and noticed a man in a gray business suit looking at a slip. Wasn't he in the dress department when she was there? Was he following her, or did he just happen to be looking for a gift for his wife or girlfriend? She would keep an eye out for him.

After she paid for the lingerie, she glanced at her watch and noticed it was close to one. She hurried outside and caught a cab to Maude's Tea Room. When she reached the tea room she saw Elna wave at her through the plate glass window.

"It's about time you showed up," Elna said when she sat down at the small table.

"You know me when I shop," Allison said. "Time passes by and before I know it, I'm late to whatever."

A waitress appeared beside them and handed Allison a menu. "I see your friend has arrived," she said to Elna. "Are you two ready to order now?"

"Yeah, she finally got here and I'm starving," Elna said. "I think I'll take the chicken and fruit salad and another glass of iced tea."

Allison handed the menu back to her and said, "I'll have the same."

"What did you buy?" Elna asked, after the waitress left. "I see you have packages from Marshall Field's."

"Some cosmetics and this!" Allison pulled the gown out of the sack.

"It's lovely, but what's the occasion?"

"It's a gift to me to make me feel good after all of the trauma I've been through."

"Okay, start at the beginning and tell me your great adventure."

"First, I want to know if you can go shopping with me tomorrow. I need to buy new summer clothes. I'm tired of all of my old ones."

"Sure I will. That'll be fun."

At that moment the waitress arrived with their food. She smiled at them as she placed the dishes on the table and said, "I hope you enjoy your lunch."

"It looks delicious," Elna said.

After the waitress left, Allison glanced at Elna and asked, "Do you mind if I thank God for this food?"

Elna looked surprised, but said, "Go ahead," and bowed her head.

After the prayer, Allison started at the beginning with her visit to the lawyer. She paused every once in a while to eat a bite. When she told about the murder that she had witnessed, Elna gasped and exclaimed, "No wonder you seemed so upset when you came after Corley!"

Allison glanced out the window occasionally as she talked. Most of the people walked by as if they had someplace to go. She noticed a man buying a newspaper at a stand across the street. Instead of tucking it under his arm and walking on, he opened it and stood with his back resting against the building while he read. She looked closely, but couldn't tell if he was the same man she had seen at the department store. He wore a gray suit, but so did a lot of other men.

Elna was so caught up in the tale that she didn't notice Allison's interest in the scene from the window.

When the waitress brought their checks, Allison was tempted to buy a take-out sandwich for the man. Wouldn't he be surprised to know that she suspected him of following her? He could be an undercover policeman sent to guard her. Then again, he might be from the Mafia. She shuddered. When she got home, she would call Detective MacDonald and inform him about the man. Meanwhile, she would ask Elna to help her.

"Elna, do you have a few minutes?"

"Sure, what do you need?"

"See that man standing on the corner reading a paper?"

Elna looked out the window and said, "Yeah. What about him?"

"It may be my imagination, but I think he has been following me."

"Oh," gasped Elna, "maybe I should go home with you."

"No, stay here until after I'm gone and watch him. If he leaves right away, call me when you get home."

"Shouldn't we call the police?"

"I'll call them from home after you call me."

It wasn't long after Allison reached home until the telephone rang. She picked it up and said, "What did you find out, Elna?"

Doug's voice asked, "Who's Elna?"

Allison's heart leaped with happiness when she heard his voice. "Oh, Doug! It's so good to hear you. Is Corley there?"

"Yes, he's here and anxious to talk to you. Corley, your mama wants to say 'Hi' to you."

"You come home, Mama?"

"Soon, Honey. In a few days Grandpa will come on an airplane and I'll pick him up. Maybe he'll come with me to Oak Grove. Won't you be glad to see him?"

"Yes. I tell Joe Grandpa come here."

Doug came back on the line. "Corley is excited about his grandpa coming. I'll have to convince him that he must wait a few more days. I miss you, sweetheart and am as eager to see you as Corley is."

"I miss you both," she replied with a sigh.

"If it's okay with you I'll bring Corley to Chicago in time to go to the airport with you to pick up your father."

Allison was touched by his thoughtfulness. "That would be wonderful, Doug. Can you take off from work that long?"

"Dr. Newberry said he would take over my patients' care while I'm gone."

They talked a few more minutes, and then Doug asked, "Who's Elna?"

"She's a friend of mine and was supposed to get some information for me. It isn't anything important. Just one of those girl things. I'm looking forward to seeing you and Corley in a few days."

After they had said their goodbyes and hung up, the phone rang again. This time it was Elna.

"Well, you were right," she said. "He folded his newspaper and took a cab right after you left."

"I'd better hang up and call Detective MacDonald. Thank you for your help."

Allison called the number that the detective had left with her. She talked to Detective MacDonald and he reassured her that it was her imagination. "Dom Giovanni doesn't know that you are the witness," he said.

But Allison still wasn't sure. If it wasn't a policeman following her, who was it?

Chapter XXIX

After Mac hung up the telephone, he called Dirk over to his desk and said, "Mrs. Ames thinks someone followed her today. I don't really think anyone did, but we can't be too sure. I'm sending someone to watch her apartment tonight. She didn't see you while she was here, so I want you to go there in the morning and follow her. Observe if anyone seems to take an interest in her activities."

"Okay, Mac. I'll be there and keep my eyes peeled. If anyone's following her, I'll be right behind him."

"If you're certain he's after her, pick him up for loitering—or any other excuse. We'll find out if he is in Giovanni's gang."

"Gotcha!"

*****

Around ten o'clock the next morning, Allison took a cab to Elna's apartment. She hoped she wouldn't have that weird feeling that she was being followed again today. Detective MacDonald didn't think Dom Giovanni knew she was the witness against him. Besides the man was in jail. Why didn't that make her feel safe? She shrugged her shoulders and rang Elna's apartment bell.

"Come in. Be ready in a minute," Elna said as she buzzed her in.

Elna's apartment faced the front of the building. Allison walked over to the window and looked out at the street below. Everything appeared normal. The traffic flowed by uninterrupted. No one walking appeared interested in this apartment house.

She turned around as Elna came into the room.

"Do you still think someone might be after you? I thought you said the detective you talked to didn't think so."

"I know, but I still can't shake off the impression of being watched. If you're ready, let's go. I'm excited about shopping for new clothes."

"And I'm happy that I can help you. Maybe I'll find something that I can't live without."

"Shall we order a cab?"

"No, I'll take my car."

Allison's spirit lifted as they drove to Marshall Field's. However, when they entered the parking garage she involuntarily shuddered. Even though it was a different one, the dark and gloomy interior brought back memories of the murder she had witnessed.

Elna noticed her trembling and said, "Come on, let's hurry out of here and you'll feel better."

When they came out into the bright sunshine, Allison shook off the painful remembrances and became excited about shopping.

They spent the next hour trying on dresses. Allison bought two summer dresses along with fashionable lingerie. Elna found a blue dress that matched her eyes and looked good with her ash-blonde hair.

The next department had casual clothes. Allison chose several shorts and shirts and a couple of sun-dresses. In the shoe department she found sandals, dress shoes, and two new purses.

"You'd think that my apartment closet was empty by looking at the number of things I bought," she said with a laugh.

"Let's cross the street to that Italian restaurant. I'm in the mood for pasta."

"Good idea!"

Several people stood behind them at the curb as they waited for the light to change. Suddenly Allison felt pressure from behind. She felt as if the crowd was pushing her into the oncoming traffic! At that moment the light changed and the cars stopped. She whirled around in time to see two men edging out of the crowd. A large, burly man held the arm of a small, thin man. The people directly behind her had curious expressions on their faces as they turned around to watch them. Others appeared unaware of anything happening. Did she imagine someone pushing people against her back?

Talking enthusiastically about their purchases, Elna didn't notice how subdued Allison had become until they entered the restaurant. When they were seated at one of the red-checked covered tables and had given their orders, she asked, "What are you so quiet about, Allison?"

"I must have imagined it, but at the stop light I felt pressure from the crowd as if someone was trying to push me into the traffic."

"Did you see who it was?"

"Two men were leaving and one of them held the other's arm. Other than that, it all seemed normal. Do you think I imagined it?"

"I don't know, but you'd better call that detective."

"He already thinks I'm either crazy or have fantasies."

*****

Lt. MacDonald sat at his desk filling out a report when Sgt. Dirk brought a man through the door. "This little rat forcibly pushed against the crowd at a stop light. He tried to shove our witness into oncoming traffic. I collared him just in time and then the light changed. She didn't suspect a thing. We'll fingerprint him and I.D. him, but I know who he is. Jock Limke. He belongs to Dom Giovanni's gang alright."

"We'll take care of him from here. You get back and keep following Mrs. Ames. Dom Giovanni must know that she is the witness after all."

*****

When Allison reached her apartment later in the afternoon, she excitedly pulled her pretty new clothes out of the boxes and bags and admired them. Tomorrow she would begin to pack for the move to her father's house in Evanston. Although she would miss the lake view, she would be glad to be away from Chicago.

The phone rang. She picked it up hoping it was Doug again.

"Mrs. Ames," Allison's heart sank. It was Lt. MacDonald. "We had you followed today. Our man caught a Giovanni gang member trying to shove you into the oncoming traffic at a stop light. We suspect they will try something else so we have a man outside your apartment to watch out for you. You would be safer in the witness protection program. Will you agree to that?"

"Oh, no! I did feel the crowd pushing in on me. If only I had stayed out of this whole affair! I can't go into a witness protection program. I've heard about them and I'd rather take my chances here. My father is coming home in a few days and I must be here to meet him."

"We can't force you into it, but we'll do what we can to protect you. Your testimony is important to the case against Giovanni. He has done so many evil things that we must get him off the streets permanently."

Chapter XXX

The next day Allison rented a car so she would have transportation to carry her personal items to her father's house in Evanston. She spent the day packing and sorting Corley's and her clothes. The ones they didn't need she put in bags for the Salvation Army, and the rest she boxed and placed in the car trunk. A few pieces of furniture that she wanted to keep were picked up by a storage company. The Salvation Army collected the remainder.

Two days later the apartment was bare. Before she had the phone and utilities discontinued, she called Lt. MacDonald and told him she was moving to her father's house in Evanston.

On the way to Evanston, she stopped at the Pet Hotel for her father's cat, T.C., short for Top Cat. The gray and white cat greeted her with loud yowls. She picked him up, and he clung to her.

"Ouch, T.C.!" she scolded him as his claws dug into her shoulder.

"Ought to let me declaw him," Mr. Hobbs, the owner said. "Save on furniture at home, also."

"No. My mother wouldn't do that to her cats, and now that she's gone, I'm going to respect her wishes."

Mr. Hobbs put him in the carrying case and placed it on the back seat. The cat meowed loudly all the way home, at first belligerently and then piteously.

"Shut up, T.C.," Allison said. "It's not going to do you a bit of good, and you're getting on my nerves!"

When she arrived at her father's two-story brick home, she was shocked. A recent wind storm had broken off a huge branch on a tree next to the house, and it had fallen against the balcony outside her parents' bedroom, nearly shattering it.

She called a tree removal company, and they said they could be out that afternoon. Next, she called the carpenter, John Ambrose, whom her father hired when he needed work done. Mr. Ambrose said it would be two days before he could get to it. Since it would be another five days before her father came home, she agreed to wait.

T.C. cautiously stalked the house, making sure no intruder had usurped his place while he was gone. Allison put away the few groceries that she had bought on the way over. Martha, her father's housekeeper, would come in the morning to help her dust and clean. It was stuffy in the closed-up house, so she raised several windows.

The ringing of the telephone surprised her. She thought it must be Detective MacDonald.

"Hello," she said.

"Hi, Sweetheart." It was her father.

"Dad, where are you?"

"I'm in New York City. Since my plane ticket isn't until Monday, I'll rest here and maybe look around a bit. How's Corley? Did you look up your birth mother?"

"Yes. I went to see the lawyers that handled the adoption and found that she had passed away. Corley and I visited the town in Oklahoma where she was born. While I was there Corley became very ill. He had pneumonia." She went on to describe in glowing terms how the doctor had saved his life. But to keep him from worrying, she neglected to tell him about the murder she had witnessed.

While she talked on the phone, T.C. rubbed against her legs.

After she hung up the phone, she patted the cat's head and asked, "Are you hungry, T.C.?" She went into the kitchen to open a can of cat food. The sound of the can-opener immediately brought him to her side. He rubbed against her legs until she placed his full dish on the floor.

After eating a light lunch, she went outside to pick up papers and other trash that had blown against the house. The men from the tree removal service came and hauled away the branch and all the loose twigs.

Mrs. Chubbs, the next door neighbor, saw Allison and came outside and said, "Hello, Allison. Is Mr. Corley coming back soon?"

"Yes, I'm picking him up at the airport Monday."

"We didn't know what to do about that tree branch. Tried to call you several times, but you were never home."

"I've been visiting friends in Oklahoma," she told her.

"We miss your mother. She was a good friend and neighbor."

"Thank you," Allison said.

Back in the house, she went upstairs to her old bedroom and made the bed, unpacked her suitcase, and put her things away. The telephone rang. It was Lt. MacDonald. "Mrs. Ames," he said, "bad news. Dom Giovanni is out on bail. The judge said we don't have enough evidence to hold him on murder charges. Somehow Giovanni found out that you're the witness to the murder. However, there is a detective in a car in front of your house, night and day."

"Isn't this nightmare ever going to end?" Allison asked.

"I'm sorry," he replied. "I know this is hard on you. We do need your testimony, though. Are you sure you don't want to be in protective custody?"

"No! I haven't changed my mind about that. In five days my father will fly into Chicago. I can't be gone when he arrives."

Allison noticed a car across the street and figured it was the policeman sent to protect her.

At eight p.m. the door chimes sounded. Allison jumped at the unexpected sound. She trembled as she crossed the room to the door and called, "Who's there?" Peering through the peep-hole in the door, she saw a man. He held up a police badge and said, "Mrs. Ames, I'm Sgt. Wilkowski."

With a feeling of relief, she opened the door. The detective came in and said, "The policeman who was here all day has gone. I'll be out front in my car if you should need me. About every half hour or so I'll walk around your house and check the windows and doors."

Allison thanked him and told him she felt safe with him there.

Before she went to bed that night, she prayed for the Lord's protection. It gave her comfort and peace until, as she was about to doze off, she heard a sudden bumping noise. There was a scratching on her door, and T.C. meowed. Cautiously she opened the door and saw that he had knocked over her empty suitcase. She had left it outside the door to take to the basement in the morning.

"T.C.!" she said, "I thought cats were supposed to be agile and not go around knocking things over. Well, you can stay in here and keep me company tonight."

The rest of the night was without incident, except once she woke up with a weight on her feet. It was T.C.! She put him off the bed, but he jumped back on and slept against her back until morning. He awakened her early by scratching and meowing at the door to get out.

She had eaten her breakfast and was ready to start the house cleaning by the time Martha rang the doorbell. A large buxom woman with iron gray hair and large blue eyes, Martha had been with the family for ten years. During the illness of Allison's mother, she had been both housekeeper and nurse, and Allison was grateful for that reason.

"Martha, I'm glad you're here. We have a lot of work ahead of us. Did you bring your suitcase to stay?" Allison asked, looking out the door.

"No, Miss Allison, I can't stay nights yet. My daughters are both visiting me for a few days, but I'll move back in as soon as they leave."

"That'll be fine, Martha. Dad won't be here until Monday, and I'll be staying awhile with him. After we get the house cleaned, you won't need to come back until your daughters leave."

"Where's Corley?" Martha asked.

"He's staying with friends in Oak Grove, Oklahoma. A friend will bring him here Friday."

"I didn't know you knew anyone in Oklahoma."

"Neither did I until two and a half months ago. Let's get started with the house cleaning, and I'll tell you all about it over lunch."

After Martha left late that afternoon, Allison looked around with satisfaction. The house was swept clean, the furniture was dusted and polished, the kitchen and bathrooms were scrubbed and waxed, and the glass in the windows, doors, chandeliers, and mirrors sparkled.

"T.C., I'm tired, but it's a good feeling to sit back and admire a job well done," she said. "After supper, I'm going to bed, and I don't want you to bother me. You got me up too early this morning."

The door chimes sounded and, after looking through the peephole, Allison opened the door to Sgt. Wilkowski. "Just wanted to let you know that I'm here again to watch your house for the night, Mrs. Ames."

"Would you like a cup of coffee?" she asked.

"No, thanks. I have a thermos in the car," he responded.

Allison took a long, hot shower and put on her nightgown and robe before going down to the kitchen. She had a light meal of fruit and yoghurt with a glass of iced tea.

On the way to her room, she picked up a magazine and took it upstairs to read. Before she got in bed, she looked out the front window and saw the detective's car across the street. It reassured her that he was there. The knowledge that he walked around the house, checking windows and doors about every half hour during the night, comforted her.

It didn't take long for her to get sleepy. With a sigh, she put the magazine aside, turned off the light, and snuggled down in the bed.

She was nearly asleep when she was jerked awake by a slight noise. It sounded like the tinkling of breaking glass. She wasn't sure if she had really heard it or just imagined it. Then T.C. scratched on the door and meowed.

She put on her robe and went to the door.

"T.C.," she said sternly, picking him up. "What have you done now? Did you break something? I think I'll put you in the basement so I can get some sleep."

She came around the curve of the staircase and stopped short. The front door stood open! And then she saw him. Outlined in the street light was the same short stocky figure she remembered from the parking garage. Dom Giovanni! Clutching the cat tightly, she whispered, "You!"

"Yeah, me. Ned gave me your name before he left town. I had you followed and I finally found you. I can't depend on anyone else killing you, so I came to do the job myself." The light glinted off the blade of a large knife in his hand. She screamed!

"No use you screaming. I already took care of that detective." He started to climb the stairs. Terror-stricken, she flung T.C. at him and fled up the stairs. The knife clattered to the floor, and he cursed as the cat's claws dug into his face and scalp. With a loud yowl, T.C. jumped from him and raced through the house to find a hiding place.

Allison ran into the nearest bedroom and locked the door. Frantically she picked up the phone to dial the police, but it was dead. He had cut the lines!

She could hear him cursing as he climbed the stairs. "When I get hold of you I'm going to slowly cut you to pieces," he growled.

He was outside the door! The knob moved slightly as he tried to turn it.

"You don't think a locked door is going to stop me, do you?" he yelled, and began slashing at it with the knife.

Allison watched in horror as the knife tore into the wood. She gasped in fright as a black-gloved hand came through the splintered hole and unlocked the door.

"God, help me!" she cried, and ran to the French doors that led to the ruined balcony. She jerked them open and ran out. The floorboards gave way and she started to fall through the gaping hole. Grabbing the railing, she desperately clung to it. Her heart was in her throat as she heard him race across the room. He was cursing and bellowing that he would slash her to pieces when he caught her.

Waving the knife, he burst through the doors. With one final scream, he fell through the hole and dropped to the flagstone terrace below. Allison stared down and saw his body lying in a crumpled heap.

She knew she was screaming over and over, but she couldn't stop. Lights went on next door, and Mr. Chubbs stuck his head out the window. Other lights in the neighborhood came on, and soon sirens were heard in the distance.

One of the first to arrive was Detective MacDonald who had been at the local police station discussing the case. He rushed into the bedroom followed by a uniformed policeman. The policeman held on to Mac's belt while Mac leaned forward and wrapped his arms around Allison's waist.

"Let go of the rail, Allison. I won't let you fall."

Allison said a prayer under her breath and let go. Mac safely drew her back into the bedroom. She clung to him, sobbing hysterically, while he awkwardly patted her on the shoulder.

Finally her wild sobs became gulps, and she said, "H...he killed that nice policeman who was watching over me."

A uniformed policeman came in and whispered in Mac's ear.

"Thank the Lord," Mac said. "Allison, the policeman isn't dead. They found him back of the house, unconscious. He had been hit on the head from behind and is being taken by ambulance to the hospital. Giovanni must not have meant to kill him. Just knocked him out so he wouldn't interfere with his plans."

Allison calmed down and asked, "I-is that awful man dead?"

"Yes. When he fell he landed on his knife, and it killed him."

"How did he get the front door open?" she asked. "I know I locked it."

"He cut a large hole in one of the glass panels on the side of the door with a glass- cutter, reached his hand through, and unlocked it. That's the problem with doors that have glass panels. Too easy to break in. Your father needs to get a security alarm on this house."

"I'll make sure he gets it before I leave," she said.

"Where will you stay tonight? You can't stay here."

"I'll pack a few clothes and go to a hotel."

When she came out with her suitcase, curious neighbors were milling around outside the yellow crime scene tapes. Television camera crews had arrived and were taking pictures and talking to people. Allison shrank back. She was still numbed by her traumatic experience and the flashing lights bewildered her. Mr. and Mrs. Chubbs were standing to one side, and when they saw Allison, they motioned for her to come over to them. She indicated to Lt. MacDonald that she wanted to talk to them, so the police cleared a path for her.

"Spend the night with us and we'll shut the newsmen out," Mrs. Chubbs said.

"It will be too much trouble for you," she said.

"No trouble," Mr. Chubbs assured her. "We'll go in, shut the door, and that will be that!"

Mac carried her suitcase over to their house, and she walked between the couple as cameras flashed and microphones were shoved in her face. Shaking her head at them, she went in the house with Mrs. Chubbs. Mr. Chubbs took her suitcase from Mac, shook hands with him, and firmly shut the door.

*****

Early the next morning Doug was shaving in a motel room in Joliet, Illinois. He hummed softly to himself and thought about Allison. Corley was dressed and ready, so Doug had turned on the television to keep him occupied.

"Mama!" Corley said.

"Yes, we're going to see your beautiful mama today," he replied.

"Mama, there," he said, pointing to the television.

Doug came out of the bathroom to see what he was talking about, looked at the screen, and gasped. Allison was walking between an elderly couple with cameras trained on her and microphones in her face. She had a haunted look and was shaking her head and saying nothing. He recognized the detective Gil MacDonald who was carrying her suitcase. She entered a house with the woman. The man took the suitcase from Mac, shook his hand, and went in. The door was shut in the faces of the newsmen.

Doug listened in amazement as the reporter recounted the occurrence of the night before. When he finished, Doug said to Corley, "We've got to get to your mama in a hurry. She needs us!"

Chapter XXXI

Allison awoke the next morning with the sun streaming through the window. Stretching, she turned over and opened her eyes. She looked around puzzled. The room was unfamiliar to her. Then it hit her! Last night---that horrible man! He was dead! With both of the murderers dead, surely the danger was past. And she wouldn't need to be a witness. What a relief! She paused to thank the Lord. Then she looked at the clock on the bedside table. Ten o'clock!

In the connecting bathroom she found fresh towels, soap, shampoo, and body lotion. The Chubbs' thoughtfulness caused her to feel welcome. After a long, luxurious shower she dressed and sat at the dressing-table to comb her hair.

Mrs. Chubs rapped on the door. "Allison, breakfast is ready."

"I'll be right out," she said.

As they ate, the Chubbs didn't mention the happenings of the night before. They sensed that she would rather not talk about it yet. Allison thanked them for welcoming her into their home.

The ringing of the doorbell or the phone was constant, but the housekeeper handled all the calls by telling them no one was home. Allison wished the calls would stop. She felt as if she were causing the Chubbs a lot of trouble. She came to the conclusion that she should go to a hotel and give the Chubbs a rest from them. As she started up the stairs to pack, the doorbell rang again. Dread took hold of her because she thought it was another reporter. But when she heard a familiar voice she turned around, darted past the housekeeper, and flew into the caller's arms. It was Doug!

"Whoa! I didn't expect such a vigorous greeting." Doug laughed and held her close.

Love for him welled up in her heart. How could she not have realized her great love for him?

"Mama, Mama!" Corley called from his seat in the car.

161

Doug released her and she sprinted to the car. She took Corley out of the car seat and hugged him.

From that point on, Doug took charge. He fielded the reporters' questions, stayed with her through all the police interviews, and went with her to meet her father at the airport.

Allison was as excited as Corley when her father's plane landed. She rushed into his arms as he came through the door from the ramp. They embraced, laughing and crying at the same time, until Corley's insistent tugging on them got their attention.

Her father scooped Corley up in his arms. "You've grown since I saw you last," he said.

Allison introduced Doug, and the two men took each other's measure and liked what they saw.

"I'm glad to finally meet you, Mr. Corley," Doug said.

"Call me Calvin," he said. "You must be the doctor who saved Corley's life. Allison told me about that. But she didn't mention anything about this." He took a folded newspaper from his briefcase and spread it out. On the front page was a photo of Allison, looking disheveled, coming out of her father's house on the night of the attack. The news story accompanied it in great detail.

"Let's get home and I'll tell you all about it," she promised.

Doug had helped her move back into her father's house. The carpenters had repaired the balcony and everything was back in order. Corley's crib was set up in Allison's bedroom. Doug had been staying in a hotel, but Calvin insisted on him moving into a spare bedroom in his house.

After a light supper, they sat in the living-room and Allison told her father the details of her terrible experience, beginning with the visit to the lawyer.

Corley went to sleep on his grandad's lap. Doug carried him upstairs and put him to bed. It wasn't long before Calvin followed suit. "I think I still have jet lag," he said.

When they were alone, Doug moved beside Allison on the couch. He put his arm around her shoulders and she didn't object.

"I was surprised by the greeting I received the other morning," he said. "Since our last meeting, I didn't know what to expect."

"I missed you, Doug."

"How much?"

"More than I thought I would."

"I noticed you were wearing your ring, but now it's gone."

"It was my defense against my feelings for you."

"And what are they?"

"I love you, Doug."

"Oh, Allison," he said in a choked voice. He pulled her into his arms and kissed her passionately. When he released her he said, "I've waited a long time to hear those words from your lips. Will you marry me?"

"I don't know."

"You don't?"

"It's the same old problem. Will the Ashley's accept me as their granddaughter?"

"Of course they will. They love you and Corley. They would've kept Corley the whole time you've been gone if you had asked."

"Let's not plan anything until I go back to Oak Grove and tell them."

"Okay. I'll be praying about it. But I know they will accept you."

Allison wasn't so sure.

Chapter XXXII

Two weeks later on a Sunday morning, Allison sat in the Oak Grove Baptist Church. She scarcely heard the sermon. She was nervous about telling the Ashleys that she was their daughter's illegitimate child. Her whole future depended upon their acceptance of her. Sleep had eluded her for most of the night. When she had finally dozed off around four a.m., it was not a restful sleep.

She and Corley had flown into the small airport the day before. Doug had driven back two weeks ahead of them, but she had stayed longer to visit with her father. Meg had volunteered to go with her to the Ashleys this afternoon.

From his seat in the choir loft, Doug smiled at her often. She loved him so much, but she didn't want him to have to leave Oak Grove because of her. It was such a nice, friendly town that she would like living here the rest of her life. But how could she if, after knowing who she was, the Ashleys didn't want to claim her? It would embarrass them every time they saw her, and it would be awkward for her also.

After the church service Doug came to Allison and said, "Be brave, sweetheart. Have faith in God. He wants the best for both of us. I will be praying for you this afternoon, and I know it will be okay. My parents wanted to invite you to dinner, but I knew this wasn't the right day. They suspect my feelings for you, and they want to get to know you."

"I wish I had been able to tell my grandparents on that terrible Friday when I had my courage built up. Now the realization of my love for you has made it more important than ever for them to accept me. If only I had as much faith as you."

All through Sunday dinner at the Sullivans, Allison toyed with her food. She noticed Meg had trouble eating, also. She's dreading it as much as I am, Allison thought.

After she put Corley down for his nap, she found Meg alone in the kitchen.

"Meg, I know you don't really want to go with me," she said, "but I need you."

Meg put her arm around her and said, "I'm not looking forward to it, but I truly want to help you. At Sylvia's deathbed I promised her that I would be there for you when you needed me."

After Corley's nap, Meg called the Ashleys and told them that she was coming with Allison and Corley. They expressed their delight and said she was welcome.

When they pulled into the drive of the large white house, Allison said, "Please go in first and tell them, and then if they don't want us, we can just drive away, and I'll go back to Chicago. Take the pictures and the letter from my mother with you."

"All right," Meg said, "but let's have prayer first." They held hands and bowed their heads. Meg asked the Lord to be with her and give her the right words to say.

Corley had bowed his head, and when Meg finished praying, he said, "Amen" and started to get out with Meg, but Allison held him back. He couldn't understand why he and his mother weren't getting out, too.

"We'll let Meg go first, and then we'll surprise them," she said. Corley laughed and agreed. He always liked surprises and thought it would be fun.

Mrs. Ashley came to the door and said, "Hello, Meg. Where are Allison and Corley? Isn't that them in your car? Why don't they come in?"

"Allison wanted me to tell you something first, and then if you still want them to come in, they will."

Mr. Ashley entered the living-room and heard the last remarks.

"That's strange," he said, "Of course we want them to come in. What happened with those bad men wasn't her fault."

"Please sit down and let me explain."

After they were seated side by side on the couch, Meg sat in a chair facing them and plunged right in, "Allison is Sylvia's daughter."

They sat in stunned silence.

Finally Mrs. Ashley found her voice to say, "Why are you saying such a thing to us, Meg? That's impossible!"

"I told you that Allison was the daughter of a friend in Oklahoma City, which was a half-truth. Allison's mother was my friend in Oak Grove as well."

"I don't believe you," Mrs. Ashley said. "Sylvia would have told us if she was married."

"She wasn't married," Meg replied, and her heart sank as she looked into those two stony faces.

"Sylvia was a good, moral person. She wouldn't do that," Mrs. Ashley said. "Isn't that right, Arlan?"

Arlan nodded his head, too heartbroken to do more.

"Yes, Sylvia was a good, moral person," Meg agreed. "She was tricked into thinking the man intended to marry her. Let me tell you how it happened," and she told them the whole story about the trip to Dallas. "He was a tall, handsome man with black hair and brown eyes, and Sylvia was too much in love to use good judgment."

"Why didn't she tell us she was in the baby way?" Mrs. Ashley cried.

"She knew it would distress you, and also her reputation would be ruined if she lived with the baby here in Oak Grove. Since she couldn't support herself and a baby on her own, she made the only choice left to her—a home for unwed mothers in Chicago and placement of the baby for adoption."

"Did you know this all along?" Mr. Ashley asked.

Meg hung her head. "She told Sue, Amy, and me and pledged us not to tell anyone else. And we didn't."

"Why are you telling us now?" he asked.

"Two years ago when Sylvia found out she had cancer, she told me to tell you if Allison ever came here seeking her."

"Why didn't she tell us at that time?" Mrs. Ashley asked. "And why didn't Allison contact us when she first came here?"

"Sylvia didn't know if Allison would ever look her up, so she didn't see any point in giving you heartache. Allison was afraid the killer would find her if he got Sylvia's address, and she didn't want to put you in danger either."

"If she could have children, why didn't she and Bernie have any?" Mrs. Ashley asked.

"After Allison was born, she had complications and had to have a hysterectomy. I didn't know that until Sylvia told me two years ago. That was why she didn't marry sooner. Bernard already had children and didn't want more at his age, so she married him and was happy."

Tears gathered in Mrs. Ashley's eyes and ran down her cheeks unbidden. "My poor baby," she sobbed. "She went through all of that by herself. I wish I could have been there for her. Did she get to see the baby?"

"Yes, she got to hold her in her arms once. She said that she was a beautiful baby with black hair and big, dark eyes. The adoptive parents sent a picture of Allison every year on her birthday, through the lawyers. Here they are. Sylvia had told Bernard to give them to me after she died."

The Ashleys sat on the couch looking at the pictures together. Mrs. Ashley was sobbing, and Mr. Ashley kept brushing the tears from his eyes. He took his handkerchief out of his pocket and blew his nose a few times.

When they finished looking at the pictures, Meg wordlessly handed them the letter that Sylvia had written for Allison. The ring fell out when Mr. Ashley took the letter out of the envelope, and Mrs. Ashley picked it up and looked at the initials inside. They silently read the letter together, both of them wiping their eyes as they did so.

When they finished reading it, Mr. Ashley looked at Meg and said, "Tell our grandchildren to come in."

Chapter XXXIII

On a beautiful fall day in October, Allison woke up in her grandparents' house in Oak Grove. She was happy and excited. Today she would become the wife of Dr. Douglas Gregory. Her champagne satin wedding gown hung on a hook over her closet door. Since it was her second wedding, she chose a simple, formal-length dress with long straight lines. A matching satin caplet with a small veil perched on a hat stand on the dresser. Her bouquet of mixed fall flowers would arrive later.

This afternoon, after the wedding and reception, they would drive to Shreveport, Louisiana, to spend the first night, and then down to New Orleans for a day and a night. Their reservations at a seaside resort in Miami, Florida, were not for another five days so they had plenty of time to get there.

For a few minutes she lay in bed stretching and thinking about how much she loved Doug. She realized her love for him that day in Evanston when he and Corley came to the Chubb's house.

Later, her father had come to Oak Grove to meet the Ashleys. With tears in his eyes he had told them how much Allison had meant to his wife and himself.

Now, he was here again for the wedding and Elna had come with him. All of Doug's family had arrived. Meg's brother, Dr. Bob Mitchell, his wife Amy, and their three pretty petite blonde teenage daughters would be at the wedding, also. They were home on furlough from the mission hospital in the Philippines. He had agreed to take over Doug's practice while he was on his honeymoon. Doug had shown Bob around his office and had taken him to the hospital to meet the staff and his patients.

Allison's grandmother knocked on her door. "Are you up, Allison?" she asked. "Breakfast is nearly ready."

"Go ahead and eat," she said. "I want to run first."

168

She quickly got up and dressed in sweats. The wedding was to be at two in the afternoon, and she had plenty of time this morning for an hour's run in the park. If only Doug could be with her now. They had run together frequently in the early morning hours during the summer. Doug's practice gave him little time for her, but what time they could spend with each other was treasured. Love between them grew stronger every day as they became better acquainted. Without the constant threat of the killers hanging over Allison, she was able to relax and become the stable person she had always been. It was a beautiful summer of discovery and delight in each other, and today their love would at last be fulfilled in marriage.

When Elna heard that Allison intended to run, she said, "I'll go with you," and quickly donned her sweats.

As they ran in companionable silence, Allison thought about her grandparents. They lavished all the love that they had had for Sylvia on her and Corley. However, they learned from their mistakes not to demand too much perfection and not to smother them with their love. Frequently, her grandmother asked her to trust them with any problem she had, and assured her that they would always be there for her and Corley.

On the way back to her grandparents' home, they stopped and looked at her future home. It was a large white, well-built older house, with a huge yard. The furniture, chosen with love and care, was in place. The day that Elna and her father arrived, she had taken them through it. Allison was glad it was located near the Ashley's home so that when Corley became a little older he could walk over to see them by himself.

The rest of the family had finished breakfast when they returned, and, while Elna helped herself to the breakfast laid out for them, Allison took only toast and orange juice. Upstairs in her room she showered and lay down to rest. The unopened presents were stacked in a corner. She and Doug would open them together in their new home when they returned from their honeymoon. Gifts she received at her bridal shower were already opened and arranged in their house.
*****

Excitement reigned that same day in the Sullivan household. Meg was to be the matron of honor and Joe the best man. Allison's wedding colors were rose and champagne, so Meg made a formal-length, rose-colored gown to wear. It had a sweetheart neckline and a long, slightly flared skirt. Joe was dressed in a rented black tuxedo with a rose-colored cummerbund.

"I feel stupid in this monkey suit," he complained.

"You look very handsome, though," Meg replied, kissing him.

The children were dressed in their best, also. Meg had sewed new dresses for the girls, and the boys wore their suits. Mike and Luke came home over the weekend for the occasion. Mike tied his long hair in a pony-tail.

"I think Allison should have waited and married me after I graduated from the university," he complained.

"Don't be silly, Mike," Sarah said. "She's too old for you. Besides I think they make a beautiful couple!"

"Ha!" Sammy said. "I'm sure Dr. Doug would thank you for calling him beautiful."

"Oh, you know what I mean," she said.

*****

The Gregory household was also filled with excitement. Sue and Sandy and their four youngest children were there. The oldest two were attending college in Berkeley, California, and couldn't take time off, but promised they would be in Oak Grove at Christmas with the rest of their family and would meet Allison at that time. Thad, along with his redheaded wife, Angie, and their two sons and young daughter were staying with Angie's parents, Burt and Opal Lester. They came over to go to church with his family. Thad also wore a rented tuxedo with a rose-colored cummerbund. He was to be a groomsman for his brother. Tammi, their four-year-old daughter, was to be the flower girl. Her curly red hair bobbed about as she skipped joyfully around the house in her champagne satin dress with the bouffant sleeves and rose-colored sash. Lace and rosebuds trimmed her full skirt.

"I still can't believe that my youngest brother is marrying Sylvia's daughter," Sue said. "When we were in high school we never could

170

have imagined this happening. She is beautiful. Sylvia would be so proud of her."

*****

The wedding took place on the church lawn because the small sanctuary could not hold all of the invited guests. A bower of colorful fall flowers was erected for the ceremony, and extra folding chairs had been borrowed from the Methodist church and the Community Building.

Arlan and Ella Ashley were seated on the left side of the aisle. The first two seats were saved for Allison's father and her son. Corley would bear the ring on a pillow, while Tammi would carry a basket of rose petals.

Arlan took Ella's hand, and they smiled at each other. Ella wondered if he were thinking the same thoughts as she. The last four months with Allison and Corley had brought them so much joy. Sylvia, the "perfect" daughter, had had a child out of wedlock, and the world had not come to an end. Their friends had accepted the fact that Allison was Sylvia's daughter and asked no questions. There may have been gossip around town by small-minded people, but they didn't care. God had forgiven Sylvia, so why shouldn't others? She only regretted that Sylvia had not trusted their love enough to let them help her. It was their own fault, because they had expected too much from her. She looked at Doug waiting by the bower, and she was happy for Allison. He was handsome, a good doctor, and best of all, a dedicated Christian. Also, she was pleased because they would remain in Oak Grove.

Doug's best man, Joe Sullivan, and Thad, his groomsman and brother, stood beside him.

The musician at the small portable organ began the wedding march. A hush came over the guests as Elna in a pale pink gown carrying a small bouquet of roses came slowly down the aisle. Meg in her rose dress, also carrying a small bouquet of matching roses, slowly followed her. Joe, standing at the front next to Doug, thought her beautiful, with her dark hair and bright blue eyes, and his love for her filled him. Next came Tammi, strewing rose petals along the path, and Corley, in a champagne satin suit with a serious expression on his face, carefully carrying the ring on a champagne satin pillow.

As Allison made her appearance on her father's arm, Ella rose, followed by the rest of the wedding guests. "Ohs" and "ahs" swept through the crowd as she came down the aisle. Doug smiled at her. Love and happiness swelled in his heart. She was so beautiful, and yet modest and vulnerable. He rejoiced that he had waited all of these years for the Lord's perfect wife for him.

The wedding went smoothly except for one hitch. The ring slid off the pillow. Joe waited with outstretched hand until Corley found it on the ground and handed it to him.

At the close of the ceremony, Meg sang "The Lord's Prayer."

After all of the photos had been taken, the bride and groom along with their parents and attendants stood in a receiving line. Allison had sent invitations to all of the hospital staff, including Nick Nichols. He had taken the news of her engagement well. Before she could tell him, he had phoned to wish her much happiness.

"How did you know?" she had asked.

"A hospital is like a small town. News flies faster than a teletype machine. Dr. Gregory is so happy that he smiles at everyone. We aren't used to seeing him so cheerful. Well, if I can't marry you, he'd be my second choice. I mean for you – not for me," Nick had said with a laugh.

She noticed him among the guests. He hung back and came through the line last. He wished her happiness and congratulated Doug. After he was introduced to their parents and attendants, he took Elna by the arm and led her away talking to her.

Allison smiled and said to Doug, "So that's why he came last! Same old Nick." Since Elna didn't know the other guests, she was glad that he was taking care of her. The bride and groom cut the cake and toasted each other with the punch and the guests were invited to partake of the refreshments. Nick gallantly escorted Elna to the buffett and then to a small table for two.

At the end of the lovely garden reception, before Allison left to change clothes, she tossed her bouquet over her head to the single women gathered together for this ritual. Elna caught it and blushed when Nick called out, "That a girl, Elna!" When they came out of the church in their traveling clothes, a shower of rice greeted them. Joe had brought the green Buick around in front of the church. It was decorated with paper streamers, and the windows were soaped with wedding messages.

"I'm innocent!" Joe said.

"Oh, no!" Doug said. "I wondered why all you children were giggling so much."

He helped Allison in, and, although they had already discussed with Corley that he would stay with his grandparents, he started to cry, holding his arms up to Allison.

"Oh, dear," Allison said, looking ready to cry with him.

"Hey, Corley, let's go get some ice-cream," Joe said.

"Okay," Corley decided and smiled through his tears as he took hold of Joe's hand, waved at his mother, and said, "Bye-bye."

When the car was out of sight, Joe picked him up and whispered in his ear, "Let's get out of these sissy clothes and go to the Freezer Queen."

Epilogue

The night of Allison's and Doug's wedding, Joe lay in bed, leaning on one elbow, watching Meg as she brushed her hair.

"Allison was such a beautiful bride," Meg said, "and Doug looked so handsome in the tuxedo. Not as handsome as you, though," she added, turning around to look at him. "I could barely keep from laughing when Corley dropped the ring. He was so serious, down in the grass searching for it. Little Tammi was so proud and looked so cute. Nick didn't waste any time latching onto Elna. Maybe something will come of this. They seemed to have fun together. Did you notice how happy the Ashleys appeared? They're glad that Allison and Corley will stay here in Oak Grove. It was a picture-perfect wedding! What do you think?"

"I think you had better get in bed and let me kiss you."

She put her brush down and slipped in beside him. "I hope they'll be happy, and their marriage will be as good as ours," she said.

"Nothing can be this good," Joe said and kissed her.

The End

Printed in the United States
1516400003B/1-84